Racket

Racket

New Writing Made in Newfoundland

EDITED BY LISA MOORE

BREAKWATER
P.O. Box 2188, St. John's, NL, Canada, A1C 6E6
WWW.BREAKWATERBOOKS.COM

Copyright © 2015 Lisa Moore

LIBRARY AND ARCHIVES CANADA CATALOGUING IN PUBLICATION
Racket : new writing made in Newfoundland / edited by Lisa Moore.
ISBN 978-1-55081-609-9 (paperback)
1. Short stories, Canadian (English)--Newfoundland
and Labrador. 2. Canadian fiction (English)--21st century.
I. Moore, Lisa Lynne, 1964-, editor
PS8329.5.N3R33 2015   C813'.01089718   C2015-904889-3

The cover and back-cover design of *Racket* are an homage to PURITY FACTORIES LTD.
(www.facebook.com/purityfactories) and the packaging of their traditional
Newfoundland Hard Bread. Design elements used courtesy of Purity Factories Ltd.

We acknowledge the support of the Canada Council for the Arts, which last year
invested $153 million to bring the arts to Canadians throughout the country.
We acknowledge the financial support of the Government of Canada and the
Government of Newfoundland and Labrador through the Department of Tourism,
Culture and Recreation for our publishing activities.
PRINTED AND BOUND IN CANADA.

 Canada Council   Conseil des Arts   Newfoundland
for the Arts   du Canada   Labrador

Breakwater Books is committed to choosing papers and materials for our books that
help to protect our environment. To this end, this book is printed on a recycled paper
that is certified by the Forest Stewardship Council®.

Reprinted 2015

Contents

Introduction

Lisa Moore

I'M IN STOCKHOLM in a crowded market in the oldest part of the city. Pigs' heads hanging from hooks, fish on crushed ice, caviar, wheels of cheese, strings of sausage, pigeons in the rafters. There are rows of tables and I'm having lunch with a translator, a writer, and an academic. The conversation has turned to the proliferation of creative writing classes in North America, the UK, and Australia.

In Europe, apparently, creative writing programs are comparatively scarce. We are arguing about whether there is a place in the university for those programs.

The academic at our table is a literature professor at the University of Stockholm and she is pale, petite, soft spoken. She wears a cream cashmere sweater with taupe trim, and her shoes match perfectly; she has an iron-straight spine.

Behind her is an old man. Between the back of his chair and the back of her chair there is about an inch, but people keep trying to squeeze through to get to the empty chairs at the other end of the long table.

The truth is that this argument against creative writing programs infuriates me. It smells of some kind of faux-mystical idea of *talent* that suggests only a select few have the ability to tell a spectacular story and they can do it more or less without editing.

As if there are no techniques to learn, no craft to study, no sweat, no revision, no reading aloud to feel the beat of each sentence, no trying it out first on friends and acquaintances or fellow writers either in or outside of a classroom.

As if the instinctive creative imperative is never contained, or hammered down with invisible nails and screws to look—yes, absolutely—effortless.

And is anything but effortless.

As if those creative writing classrooms aren't actually secret covens where writers want to share their art as it comes into being.

Most of the writers in this anthology met in a creative writing class at Memorial University. These writers continued to meet, beyond the classroom, over a period of three years.

In fact, they're still meeting. They've actually named their group The Port Authority and in these ensuing years they've become some of the most exciting voices at work on the island.

The writers offer each other critical and editorial expertise and artistic inspiration. Fine cheese and excellent wine. Or Cheezies and bad wine, it doesn't matter—they make an audience for rough drafts and polished works. They form a community where small things, like the just-so placement of a semi-colon or a paragraph break, can lead to ferocious debate. And bigger things can lead to torrents of talk—things like the staggering emotion and profound insight required to make a great story.

I am listening to the Swedish academic speaking about the European disdain for creative writing programs in universities, and thinking about the contents of the anthology you hold in your hands. These stories are creative and sophisticated in terms of form, emotionally and intellectually affecting.

Explosive and subtle, politically and culturally aware, hilarious or treacherously dark.

Take Matthew Lewis's "The Jawbone Box": spare, imagistic writing suffused with longing and loss, elegant and understated. It is about a box of bones—jawbones—that are for sale. A travelling home inspector sees a wooden box and a sign nailed to a post on the side of the road. He is compelled to turn back and investigate. The reader intuits the mystery of these bones, the history— what makes us turn back?—and the mortality they suggest. Lewis's story is surreal and paradoxically concrete, elegiac. Beautifully and seamlessly crafted.

Or: Jenina MacGillivray's "Gorillas," a harrowing and wry story about the relationship between two sisters, one of whom is suffering from mental illness and believes she has turned into a gorilla. MacGillivray renders the tenderness between the sisters, and the tangible havoc doubt can cause. The overarching doubt of what it means to be human, or the academic doubt that troubled Descartes when he came up with the notion "I think, therefore I am"—a notion the narrator concludes is a bit of a leap! Doubt is overcome, in this story, by the inviolate love between the sisters.

The old man at the next table in the Swedish market whose chair back is nearly touching the academic's, is a stout man, spittle-exhaling, square-shouldered and silver-stubbled. He ignores the people pressing to get between the chairs. He is impervious to their desire; he is wilfully blocking the aisle. He raises a forkful of mashed potato to his mouth and he is instantly transformed, in my mind's eye, into an allegory for those against creative writing programs.

The cream and taupe academic is chirping that in France, especially, they cannot fathom the idea. In France they think all you need to be a writer is a gitane, a glass of wine, and a spark of genius.

I think of the story "Crossbeams" by Iain McCurdy. It is a joyous gush of language. The narrator describes the "unstoppable forces in the world" such as a powerful, fragile love affair, tumultuous as a Ferris-wheel ride. Language here is unstoppable too— lassoing sentences, roping in undiluted emotion. McCurdy pulls all the stops—this is pure sensation. The story illuminates the ordinary when it's touched by new love, "when you're tingling everywhere."

Certainly there are lots of sparks here, captured in the controlled burn of fine writing.

The academic brings up the cookie-cutter theory—that graduates of creative writing programs all write the same kinds of stories.

How very different McCurdy's story is from the magic realism of Melissa Barbeau's story "Holes," which describes a mythical deluge or an environmental disaster. Barbeau's magic realism conjures the city busting open and tumbling inward after an evening of dancing in a bar full of sweating bodies, wet walls, noise. Gorgeously dreamlike and urgent, Barbeau's story is an ablution; it washes over, shines. As the ground opens, leaving bottomless craters all over the city, a sensual tryst turns into a frightening encounter. Barbeau's protagonist runs away from a man who grabs her all over with crab-pincer hands until, with a violent surge of power, the young woman breaks free.

The voice and tone in Gary Newhook's "23 Things I Hate in No Particular Order" is in sharp contrast with Barbeau's torqued, nightmarish suspense.

Newhook's story is charged with anger and absurd humour. The antic narrator is volatile and nostalgic, buoyed by revenge. He is "pissed off and drunk and good and uninhibited" and he can imagine the moment when he must read the letter he's writing aloud at the next "meeting." Epistolic in form, the story is a response to court-ordered therapy and an address to an unnamed support group and a doctor. The narrator composes a list of the things he hates.

Newhook's fiction laments the "prefabricated shitboxes" taking over the farmland that has been in his narrator's family for generations and all the many losses that lead to growing up and finding oneself alone. Newhook's tone is irreverent and gleefully careening—and already we're about halfway through the anthology and there is a diversity of style and voice, even sub-genre (a story in the second person, realism, magic realism, the epistle), to dismiss the cookie-cutter theory.

Susan Sinnott's "Benched" is a heart-rending, redemptive story of a young man struggling with the decision of whether or not to undergo the amputation of a limb after an accident. Sinnott's writing is precise and as clean as an operating room, unsentimental and convincing. The possible amputation of a young athlete's limb becomes a metaphor that warns us about acceptance and change. A lesson suffused with a calibrated dread and metaphysical weight.

"Like Jewels," by Jamie Fitzpatrick, also shows a family in the wake of an accident, but in this case the death of a young single mother is at the heart of the story. Fitzpatrick shows the traces of this tragedy as it marks the lives of those left behind: shattering connections, disabling and grinding down the family, creating a palpable grief that seeps through generations. Fitzpatrick is unflinching in capturing the claustrophobia of a small town, broken relationships, poverty and family—the need to escape, and the impossibility of escape.

Carrie Ivardi also writes about escape and accident, but her story, "Rescue," is populated with young, sexy, pot-smoking, ski-bums capable of giving themselves over to love, to music, to sport, or alternatively, turning a cold shoulder and refusing to commit. Ivardi's writing is as adroit as a skier racing downhill before an avalanche. These characters are pulsing with desire, but unfettered by gravity. They pass through each other's lives, provoking thrills, skimming the surface, ultimately seeking the next ski resort, the next love, and the next sensually heightened experience.

Melanie Oates's "A Holy Show" is ripped through with dialect, humour and fear, self-loathing and drama. Here is the downtown St. John's bar scene in the wee hours, electric with errant sexual intent and potential violence. Full of "bitch fights" and spilled drinks, come-ons and threats. Here, as with Fitzpatrick's story, the particularities of voice and setting in Newfoundland are captured with authenticity. Oates portrays female vulnerability poignantly, and the opposite: a woman alone in a cold city, made vivid with the will to survive.

The sombre, stark realism of Oates's story contrasts dramatically with Morgan Murray's "KC Accidental," in which the titular character, KC, meets with an oncoming bus and is reduced to a smear on the asphalt. Murray's story is a galloping shaggy dog romp that ripples in ever-widening tangents, spilling over the rim, exploding our expectations of form (there's a list of the names of lesser-known Catholic saints that runs to half a page) and plot (corpse switching, bursting caskets, crying elementary children delivered by the busload). Murray explores the idea of contingency and consequence, and the obdurate insistence of bad luck, once it gets a hold of us. There is a new brand of fierce farce here and the comedic moments shoot out like comets, as well as insight about the ways bureaucracies botch those sacred rituals that mark our lives, including the practices for dispatching the dead.

This anthology's final story, "A Drawer Full of Guggums" by Sharon Bala, is set in contemporary London. Bala's protagonist, Cait, a Canadian student of Sri Lankan descent, is rooming with her Aunt Dodo. Cait is studying the Pre-Raphaelite painter Dante Gabriel Rossetti and his model and lover, Lizzie Siddal, for her Master's dissertation.

Just as Cait plaits Dodo's long black hair, so the various strands of Bala's story weave in and out to form a strong, gleaming braid of narrative. Rossetti's mistreatment of his beautiful lover echoes the experiences of Cait and Dodo. Past secrets are revealed as the women become dependent on each other, their lives braiding together in a delicate friendship.

Cait tries to remember the Tamil language she could speak as a child, and drinks tea from Dodo's china cups, decorated with images of Princess Diana and Prince Charles. The allegiance between the two women is based not only on the brown colour of their skin and shared cultures, but on the differences between them, in age, in colonial history, and finally, most poignantly, on their understandings of love and loneliness. Bala doesn't waste a word in capturing the complexity of these women's lives, desires, disappointments, and fears.

Back at the Stockholm market, the academic, the writer, the translator and I are just finishing our lunch. A young father with his kicking toddler in one arm and a Snugli with an infant on his chest is trying to squeeze through the inch between the back of the old man's chair and the academic's chair.

The old man, Mr. No-To-Creative-Writing-Programs, will not move.

The young father insists on nudging forward.

The academic has just finished her monologue about the cookie-cutter theory.

They say the stories are all alike.

Yes, I say. Stories that come out of creative writing classes do have something in common: the desire to be different, to push the perimeters of expression, to articulate something essential about human experience. The desire to make stories memorable. But that's about all they have in common.

Suddenly the academic, who until now has been nothing but poised and suave, combusts with fury.

Why will he not move *his* chair, she says. She's speaking of the old man. Mr. No-To-Creative-Writing-Programs. The father with the two children is now wedged tight between the two chair backs. The infant is crying.

The potato plops off the old man's raised fork and falls back onto his plate. He twists in his chair and his milky eyes behold the young man, and with great effort he rises and stumbles out of the way.

And I say what people always say about the cookie-cutter theory of creative writing classes: Engineering graduates don't all make cookie-cutter suspension bridges, but they still go to engineering school.

Yes, there might be something called talent or genius (I would call it the need to tell a story, the absolute need to voice experience, as urgent sometimes as drawing breath, and the electric charge that shoots through those experiences causing a story to coalesce, or come into being, the big bang of plasma and stone and whatever, that added ingredient that makes a story vital, explosive, quaking). But without craft and technique, the story is nebulous, unsolid, melts into air. Those are things that can be studied and learned.

The stories in this collection were written by writers who continue to meet in order to hear each other's stories, to offer criticism, to laugh at the funny parts, get sad at the sad parts, to marvel at the moments of beauty and to point out where a small change might torque the whole structure; where a sentence cut, or cut and pasted elsewhere, might bring a scene to life.

But these stories could not be more different from each other—in terms of style and content.

What they have in common is excellent writing.

Craftsmanship.

I would like to thank James Langer for his editorial brilliance, and Rebecca Rose, and the whole gang at Breakwater for making this anthology possible. A special thanks to Melissa Barbeau for some eagle-eyed assistance. Thank you to Memorial University. And thank you to the writers herein for their words.

The Jawbone Box

Matthew Lewis

H

OW YOU READ the sign is, you're passing it. You're passing the sign and you have to look back to take it all in. It's tacked to a maple tree. You turn back to the road. You think about it, mull it over. The caged metal box below. The padlock. The Jawbone Box. When it finally registers, you're well past it.

It's a box for jawbones.

Now the sign did not specify. You think about it some more but there was nothing specific about the sign. The sign did not say, squirrel jawbones or moose jawbones. The sign did not say, mammalian or reptilian jawbones. Or avian jawbones.

It appeared to be, simply, a box for jawbones in general.

You are already four days travelling. Home is still a long way out. Home is a telescope in reverse. That long, distorted corridor.

In between is dirt roads, crimped roads, roads scraped clean by asphalt grinders, road blocks, construction crews. The tires whine in the corduroy grooves. In between is new towns and old towns and dead towns. The blast of plant smoke, concrete flues, steam spilling like aerosol whipped cream. The smell is palatable, organic, industrial, edible. The smell is the smell of a whole world under renovation.

Dinner is a bowl of pea soup and a fluff of pale dumpling. The dumpling looks like a scoop of ice cream with the consistency of marshmallow. The diner has six tables only. It seats exactly twenty-four people. Six plastic-wrapped tables with gingham placemats and each table has a plastic cup full of crayons. There is a bulletin board near the coffee maker that advertises last year's Christmas dance. A child-minding service with none of the numbers pulled away.

The waitress is a large, hospitable woman. She never stops moving. She sets the table in front of you, cocoons of forks and spoons together, and she sets a second spot but there is no one else and you think you must look like someone expecting company. A glass of water from a sweating jug. The slosh of ice. She pours the jug sideways, hand under the glass like a connoisseur. Can I take your order? she asks, mid-pour. The ice and water sloshing, settling. There is a towel under her arm. And a pen in her ear.

Pea soup, you say.

Homemade pea soup, she says. Good choice.

She comes back shortly, instantly, with the soup, the pale dumpling, setting it down carefully, the soup sloppy and steaming and terribly yellow and there's the faint outline of her thumbprint on the rim of bowl. You smile up at her and thank her and when she leaves you stare down into your lunch, considering it like a dare.

You eat the dumpling first with the spoon. You inspect the spoon after each bite, turning it in the light and wondering, how many mouths? There are scratch marks on the spoon. Teeth marks or the natural wear of machine-washed cutlery. Like key scrapes on a vehicle or a dog owner's hardwood. You see yourself in the gnarled reflection of the spoon and you are unrecognizable, a vagrant. You will have to shave tonight. You decide now that you will find a hair in your soup. There is always a hair in your soup. You eat guardedly, suspiciously, hoping to reinforce your view of the world.

The box appeared to be full. You think about it again and again over lunch and you know the box was full. You will pass by it again tomorrow. You will confirm the fullness of the box at this time. But for now this is all you have to go on: that it is a box for jawbones in general and it may or may not be full. And there is a padlock. The box is guarded.

Your tongue is burnt and sore from the morning's black coffee.

The jawbone box has made you intensely aware of your own mouth. You know the temperature of soup can vary tremendously and you take cautious sips as though carefulness can change the temperature of things. You have not yet found a hair in your soup.

You think of your own jawbone. Solid ivory scaffolding, rods of teeth, straps of muscle fibers like the exposed roots of oak trees. You think of other bones that belong to you. You think of words like femur and sesamoid. You do not know these words. Not really. You think that skeletons are other things, anthologies of bone. You have never considered skeletons to be anything other than medical relics. Anything other than anthropological art. Anything other than Halloween decorations, laminated cardboard with small metal hoops for joints. And you think now that there's a skeleton actually inside you, a real one, a real cartoon-looking thing folded into your flesh and muscle and you think how strange, how weird, how fucked up that there are actually skeletons folded into all of us.

The waitress is above you now and she asks how you're doing and you picture her as though she is behind an x-ray.

You say you're doing fine, thanks for asking.

You do not say you are looking for a hair.

You do not ask, Are these teeth marks?

You are an inspector of homes and buildings for an insurance company. You travel too much. The insurance company is built on a foundation of minimizing risk and you are sent to hunt for risk and to neutralize it like a form of pest control. Controlling risk is literally in your job description. You do not enjoy your job. You enjoy your job. You enjoy this pea soup. The corollary is that you see risk even when you are not looking. The burnt out fluorescent lighting is indicative of a deeper electrical issue. There are exposed bulbs over customers' heads, soups, dumplings. The crunch of glass. There is a slick of water just beyond the floor mat. The floor mat is curled and frayed on one edge like a lapping tongue and the tongue is saying, Come on, you, trip. The slick of water is like candle wax. Within it the upsidedown restaurant. Within it a thousand days or more of litigation and discoveries and physiotherapy.

You finish your soup quietly.

You do not find a hair.

You are disappointed by your stroke of luck.

You remember the next house as scraps of minutiae like a strange art exhibit, or, more appropriately, like a trailer park ravaged by a tornado. Or, an exploded puzzle. You remember the house as greased vinyl tablecloths and breadcrumbs in the margarine. You remember the house as rags of orange carpet and *Littlest Hobo* reruns on a floor model television and a long narrow hallway with station-wagon walls. You remember the kitchen table but also a second table in the living room for company and the table was a boat or a fort, it was solid, you remember, dense, and you consider now that this table was perhaps what held the home together.

You expect the house to bestow some likeness of your grand-parents onto the new owners. But there have been a long line of owners since your grandfather and grandmother and the likeness is thinned beyond any recognition. The man is young, energetic. His wife is quiet and aloof. These people are not your grand-parents. They invite you in. They call you an adjuster but you are not an adjuster. You do not adjust. You do not correct them because. Because you have stopped correcting people on this point. In insurance matters there are salesmen and there are adjusters, before disaster and after. You will always be one of these.

You recall these small exhibit scraps as you are taken through the home and you do not tell the owners that you know their house better than they do. You do not tell them you were here when the house was new. You do not tell them about the station-wagon walls or the orange carpet or that there was a boat in the living room and you guard these memories like a cantankerous curator.

In fact there is not much about the house you recognise and you are pleased that your version of things is preserved only in memory. You do not want these people to live in your grand-parents' house and you are happy to discover that they do not.

In the kitchen you look above the doorframe and there is a pinch in your heart and you recognize something, finally, a varnished pine plaque placed there by your grandfather. You were with him when he bought the knick-knack, when he nailed it there and you remember the revolving display of them at the drugstore and your grandfather studying them as though he were investing in a philosophy. The plaque reads: The older I get, the more I recall, how little I knew when I knew it all.

The owner now reads this for you, out loud, and you smile as though it is the first time you've heard it. But you're thinking instead of a different plaque. You're remembering that he bought two different plaques that day although you have not seen the second one anywhere. The plaque read: A camel can go without a drink for eight days, but who the hell wants to be a camel? Before you leave, the owner shakes your hand and you ask him, casually, with camels on your mind, the location of the nearest liquor store. But the owner tells you he does not drink and you wonder then about the fate of the second plaque and you think, here, right now, is a man who wants to be a camel.

The view of yourself in the motel mirror is startling. You drink liquor from a coffee mug, holding it like coffee while you shave. Sipping it like coffee. Sliding the razor slowly along the edge of your face, feeling your jaw as an extraneous limb.

There is hair in the sink and somehow it is not your hair.

You are afraid of it. You wash the hair away with the tap water, splashing the upper reaches of porcelain but the hair is as resilient as pubic hair on soap. You reassess yourself post-shave, still unimpressed. You wonder if there are other boxes in the world for other bones.

The hipbone box.

The tailbone box.

More rain. You try to picture other people who've stayed here. In the same squat motel room. The same bed. How many mouths? Stains on the carpet the same colour of the carpet only darker. Shades of stains, dimensions of them. The ceiling slopes with the roof. You've hit your head while changing. You've said, Fuck. You've said fuck because there are things you say when you've hit your head and this is one of them. Pain is the audience. You picture someone else at this desk, sitting. The glow from the laptop. The desk lamp with extra outlets. You could plug a lamp into a lamp. And another lamp into another until you had an infinite progression of lamps and you wonder if this is, on some theoretical level, how the world works. The curser is blinking in the Google search bar and you type:

Jawbone Box.

The rain stops suddenly and you notice the noise of cars now. Attention is demanded by abundance. The noise of them passing on the highway, not quite a hiss but a hiss with bass, a throb, a thrum, elusively bursting with meaning. Google is as confused as you are. You close the lid of the laptop. You notice you are slouched and humpbacked in the wall mirror and there is the coffee mug, full of anything. You straighten your back, sip.

On your way out of town the next day you slow to take more of the sign in. You stop altogether. You pull over. The details come into focus as though under a lens. The sign is embossed driftwood, varnished. You stare at the box below. The box of jawbones. The lid of the box is pushed open. The padlock is unlatched, hanging. The container is bursting with jawbones. They look large, cumbersome, substantial. You decide, moose. That they are the jawbones of dead moose. You can picture the noise of one jaw being added to the box. The clanking. A reanimated mouth.

There's a man who comes out of a house and he has a big green garbage bag and he's hurrying across his lawn. The bag is flapping behind him like a cape. You're sitting and minding your business and wondering about the jawbones. He taps on your window. You roll down your window. He asks you if you want to buy a jawbone. He says he saw you eying them and you were eying them, true, but you were also minding your business. More minding than eying. But there are crucial questions to be asked here. The man, for one, does not look like a purveyor of jawbones. Or maybe he does. Maybe he looks exactly how you'd imagine a bone salesman to be and you consider other sayings now. That everything is for sale at the right price. Or one man's trash is another man's… Picturing the words hung above other people's doorframes, one doorway after another, an infinite progression of drugstore philosophies, jam-packed wisdom, time-worn, hand-me-down things seared in varnished driftwood. The rain is coming down real hard now. The garbage bag is flapping in his hands. He's leaning down to get a look at you, this potential buyer of secondhand jawbones. His hand is on his hat and it looks like the rain is paining him. The Jawbone Box is behind and to the right of him, and for a moment you see it all as a still shot—a portrait of the curious salesman and his bones.

You roll up your window. You do not answer him. You are not in the market for spare jawbones. You already have one, custom-built, fully operational. He looks as confused as you are. There is not much that makes sense to you anymore. There are noises for seasons and this is one of them. Fall is the sound of rain heard from inside a vehicle.

Gorillas

Jenina MacGillivray

ANNA MAKES FORAYS into whatever wilderness she can discover existing around our house in the city. She brings a notebook, in which she draws pictures for her collection "Wild Things Existing Harmoniously With City Life." She's nimble, curly black hair, penetrating green glare. She climbs trees and looks through the leaves and observes passersby, like a bi-polar Harriet the Spy. Very often, she ends up in the graveyard. She draws a digger, digging a grave. She returns to the house with paper objects she's collected. These objects come to exist in a new reality in her presence. She says they call out to her. Scratch tickets, grocery receipts, bus transfers. Things that were formerly trees.

Anna's staying with us because her fiancé is out of town on business for a month. Sometimes the cops bring her home. This time, the tall cop who accompanies her to the front door has draped a blue blanket over her shoulders. Anna is holding on to a matchbook. It has a little blue bird on it and it says, "Blue Bird Cabs, We'll Get You Where You Need to Go."

Read this, Anna says, and holds up the matchbook. Read what this says. This is about me.

I try to do the planned ignoring. Her doctor told me to do this.

When the doorbell rang, Nate and I were in the living room, watching TV. Or, Nate was watching TV and I was watching our neighbours, through their kitchen window, cooking and drinking wine. Sometimes he reads to her and after that they make out on the couch. It's too far away for me to be able to read the titles of the books. For this I would need binoculars, which is a step I'm not willing to take.

Seems Anna had been sitting on the ground in the graveyard reading the tombstones. Someone had seen her out their window, getting her shoulders covered over in snow, and called the cops. The snow is now melting on the shoulders of the blue blanket.

She's wearing her white bathrobe.

This is your sister?

Yeah, come in, I say. I'll run a bath.

Meanwhile, Anna raises the matchbook and holds it next to her face, cocks her head to one side. She has one hand on her hip and an eyebrow raised like hello I have serious evidence here.

It's unpleasant somehow, having a revolving door in a psychiatric hospital. Holding on to my sister's coat and a black, reusable bag from the grocery store full of socks and underwear. Anna still wears her white robe with her engagement ring tucked in the pocket. I couldn't get her to put shoes on.

In a side room waiting to see the doctors and she still fingers the matchbook. She tucks it into the pocket of her robe next to the engagement ring. Then, she starts to change shape.

I'm pretty sure I'm turning into a gorilla. Am I starting to look like a gorilla?

Her movements are heavy, lumbering. Her shoulders slope. She makes her way around the room.

Planned ignoring doesn't work for circumstances like this. People changing into gorillas.

You're not a gorilla. You're human. Trust me. If you were a gorilla, you would have hair all over you, right? Do you have hair all over you?

Not as far as I know.

So you're not a gorilla. Also, you can talk. Think about it. I promise.

I use the same big sister tone and language as when we were kids. If you run really quickly back up the basement steps nothing will get you. And nothing did.

Maybe I'm a hairless gorilla who can talk, Anna says.

When we were young, our parents took us to the Washington Zoo. The gorillas lived in a large pit with trees and a mini lake. A habitat. Some bratty kid leaning over the railing threw in a pile of bright candy wrappers, yelled insults at the gorilla family. Anna and I tried to make him fall in, using only our eyes, like in that book by Stephen King. The baby gorilla knuckled over to the blue wrapper, inspecting with its brown lips. Then the mother gorilla instantly covered the ground between her and her baby with the most surprising speed for her size, took the wrapper from its mouth, glared at the child leaning over the habitat railing. An intelligent, human glare. Steady and full of resentful acceptance. The kid stopped yelling and hid his face. Anna and I high-fived.

Anna gorillas over to the other side of the empty waiting room. The door is closed and thick. She bangs on the small window with her gorilla hand. Then she's fumbling in the pocket of her robe.

Read out what it says on the bottom of this matchbook. She kicks it over to me.

Keep away from children.

That's about me. You better keep me away from your daughter.

No. It means keep matches away from children. It's not about you. I promise.

I had a recurring dream when I was a kid where I was sword fighting with my younger cousin Matthew in a large white room filled with different sized white blocks. I cut his face, and out of the long red slit, the envelope of skin I'd created, came instructions, covered in plastic: how to change your cousin back into a primate. Evolution in reverse. I peeled off layers of his skin, tissue, and muscle and he became a chimpanzee. Maybe I told Anna this dream.

Anna starts sentences with "in the wild" as in: In the wild, light is always changing. It's never a constant glare all the time. You should install a dimmer in here. She tells me about articles she's read like "Boy Raised by Wolves" and "Yorkshire Housewife Adopted by Monkeys in Jungle." She memorizes quotes in the articles and suddenly repeats bits to me as if she's reading aloud. The woman learned to catch birds and rabbits with her bare hands after being abandoned in the jungle by kidnappers, it was reported. She shows me a picture online of a pretty dark-haired woman next to a picture of a capuchin monkey.

Two nurses come in, a man and a woman, and speak to me in hushed tones.

Is she violent?

Anna turns her gorilla head toward us.

The male nurse is already moving toward Anna, places a hand on her shoulder.

The thing is, Anna will respond OK to me in this state. She

knows that I know that she's not completely gone, even when she's changing species and such. But when doctors and nurses approach her, something primal takes over. It's because when she tells them about the gorilla thing they don't believe they can appeal to rationality. They assume there is none. *How can one think one is turning into a gorilla and still be able to think rationally?* they think. Anna can see they're a little bit afraid of her and she also sees the needle held by the female nurse, and this combination of affairs releases the gorilla fully and she lets out a screech and I try to tell them she's OK, she'll be OK, but Anna is rushing the door, banging it with her gorilla shoulder and screaming like they're going to murder her. Like this, right now, is the end of her life. I try to put my arms around her, but she escapes and they inject her with the needle, the two of them holding her down.

I'm sorry, says the nurse, we have to.

Anna is admitted and says don't leave me but now that she's been sedated she's almost asleep. They have an IV set up because she's a little dehydrated.

They have to watch her closely because Anna has a bird heart. Not literally, of course. No heart transplant wherein her human heart was replaced by the heart of a robin or a chickadee. It's weak because there was a hole in it when she was born. As a baby she would periodically turn an alarming shade of blue because of the hole, so no one wanted to babysit her. My mother, convinced it would fill up the hole, began feeding Anna pabulum and potatoes in her bottle, and the doctors said yes, it does seem to be filled up. My mother had to make the hole in the end of the rubber nipple bigger with a red-hot needle. Anna says sometimes she thinks she can feel the hole in her heart. The place where the hole used to be. The phantom hole.

At home Nate is stoned and watching TV and marking papers. He asks if I want to play chess. He will slot me into the line-up. I go to bed instead and read. A few pages in and Rachel wakes up in the other room and starts wailing, so I grab her, settle in with her and read the same line of *The Meditations* over and over again. I think therefore I am. I think. I think. Descartes was looking for one thing that he couldn't doubt and decided it was thinking. So he decided he must at least be a thing that thinks. Which means he must exist.

Isn't that a bit of a leap? I ask Rachel. From thinking to being? Rachel smiles at me with her pink gums.

I think about how I want sun. I want a bath. In the bath, I want Calgon to take me away, like those commercials from the eighties.

The idea that everything is probably futile starts to sink me in the morning. I don't resist. I wade into it while I drink my coffee. I'm surrounded.

Later, a new friend wants to come in and visit Anna in the hospital. It's a mistake, even though the friend means well. It's awkward. Anna won't touch most of the food, suggests they are certainly trying to poison her. She'll eat green foods only. Green foods are OK. The salad. The Jell-O. Anna eyes my friend and asks if she's ever seen *Planet of the Apes*. My friend nods her head no and Anna eyes her even more suspiciously. Anna's constant-care nurse is a big, gentle young man with soft, light brown hair. She trusts him. When she finishes lunch he puts his hand on her arm.

Come on, my dear, he says. Come now, we goes.

A shift later that night at the bar and it's busy. A regular at the end of the bar, a local playwright and heavy drinker, yells about hating Americans. Is always the last one to leave. Nate had wanted to see one of his plays. We needed a night out together. A one-man play called *Drinking: A Love Story*. The set was a replica of the bar. The actor looked a lot like a younger version of the playwright. He wore the same kind of clothes and yelled about hating Americans for almost the whole first half of the play.

Two hours into the shift and my breasts are so hard and full of milk I have to go into the bar bathroom and sort of shoot some of it out into the toilet. It hits the water in the bowl in a cloudy line. It pings off the cold ceramic, and some of it, warm, pools in my hand.

At the end of the night my clothes stink of cigarette smoke, so I remove them just inside the front door and walk up to the bathroom and throw them in the washer. In my underwear I walk past the living room and Nate is still up. He's sitting in the red velvet armchair and a group of students lounge at his feet, smoking and staring at him in wonder. The baby cries and he looks up.

Nate has this habit of using my name as a whole sentence. As in: Jane. Pause. I'm going to do the laundry, or Jane. Pause. It's your turn to do the dishes. Sometimes I call him Tarzan. Mostly because it goes with Jane. He has soft hands. He may not survive in the wild.

I'll be in in a minute, he says.

I'm going to sleep, Tarzan. I'm beat.

The students on the floor all say goodnight in unison and it's kind of creepy. I scoop Rachel out of her crib and make a nest for her next to me in bed.

My sister's fiancé is back from his business trip and he comes in to visit her. Her gorilla walk is new to him and, frankly, it's freaking him out. He's a good guy. He's supportive. They've been together for about year. He fell for her right away because she's so smart and gorgeous. He asks why she isn't wearing her ring. She says keep me away from children.

A Polish man is selling red roses at the café and he tells me he's saving up to buy a stereo for his daughter for Christmas. His daughter lives in Poland and she's coming for Christmas and she'll stay with him in the room he lives in on Duckworth Street. It has a shared bathroom but it's clean enough, and they'll make it work and he hopes she'll be able to stay in Canada with him and get a job. He only needs to sell ten more roses and I buy them, a dollar each.

Things seem less futile today. Today it's OK that there's no enduring contentment. There's only buying your daughter a stereo for Christmas. Or making sure she doesn't choke or fall down the stairs. There's reading. There's wondering what there is that you can't doubt and thinking it's probably not just thinking. There's making love. There's music. There's reading a line of poetry or listening to another person talk and thinking I have felt that way before. That's what we have. Anna doesn't always have that. She loses the thread of what some things mean. Or she picks up a very different thread. It occurs to me that sometimes her thread is just as good or in fact better than any other thread.

The man sitting at the table next to me leans in and says I bet he doesn't even have a daughter.

I bring the roses to Anna. She's on the phone when I get there. She seems better. For example, she's wearing shoes. The thing is that now she's headed for a dark period where she'll be very down for a long time. She won't want to get out of bed for a month, maybe.

She's got the horoscopes open on her lap.

Brainstorm and aim high. Mercury is in Sagittarius today. It's OK to conjure up grand ideas.

Thanks. In fact, I'm conjuring right now.

What are you conjuring?

Grand ideas.

Such as?

Such as you should come stay at my place for a little bit.

Anna doesn't like to stay at my place because she doesn't like Nate. But her fiancé is out of town again. Besides, Anna had said yesterday that her fiancé is off the hook. I had tried to be light about it and said off the hook as in off the hook and made sort of really uncool rap hand gestures, but she said no, not off the hook in a good way.

The doctor wants to let you come home, but he says you can't be on your own right now.

Will you make risotto?

Yes, I say.

Anna links her arm in my arm.

I take Anna home with me and make mushroom risotto for everyone, me and Nate and Anna. Rachel is down for her nap. The pan is too thin on the bottom so I have to stand there and stir it for a long time so it doesn't burn, but it burns anyway so I scrape off the top layer. The burnt taste is still all through it.

Nate asks how are you feeling. Nate has eaten all the risotto on his plate even though it tastes like burn, which is kind.

Don't let little things take on more significance than they deserve, Anna says.

OK, I'll keep that in mind.

Anna tells us that our cells regenerate every seven years so it's like we're a totally new person. She talks about that small monkey found wearing a little beige seventies coat in an Ikea store in Edmonton. She describes it at the window as if it's waiting for someone to pick it up and take it on a road trip to get stoned and play the guitar and blow this pop stand.

Anna and I go for a walk downtown, take Rachel in the stroller. We walk by a huge round condo and we can make out a dog barking inside. The barking sounds like it's coming from the very center of the condo. Anna makes up a headline: Barking Dog Trapped in Center of Round Building Goes Barking Mad. She seems to be skipping the dark this time. She's going straight to the joking about it. We cut through the graveyard on Cathedral Street, holding our breath, like we did when we were kids.

I know I'm a strain on your relationship with Nate.

Yeah. You are.

So why don't you tell me to take a hike.

You mean I'm off the hook?

Yeah. You're off the hook.

I like being on the hook.

Yeah?

Yeah, pretty much.

Anna does her gorilla walk across the street and I follow her, pushing the stroller, and I call after her.

Hairless Talking Gorilla Loose Near Water Street!

Anna lumbers up the hill. She gives me a thumbs-up, with her gorilla thumb.

Crossbeams

Iain McCurdy

S HE CAME OUT of nowhere, and so did I. We met at a birthday party in April. It was a setup right from the beginning, except not with her. I was in the kitchen making conversation when the woman I was to meet came through and left again with but a passing glance. I found myself leaning against a wall, watching a production, the rumble of throat sounds in a room. Then there she was and she stopped, but didn't, if you know what I mean. She stopped so we could keep going.

There are unstoppable forces in the world; you can try and stop them, or you can become one. Sometimes out of nowhere, you can be going along minding your own business and something will happen, and another thing will happen, and a string of things that all had to happen, just so, impossibly, take you somewhere, unexpectedly. Magically the stars line up for your every step, and you can never be sure it'll ever happen again. It happens though; there are many stars. But it's another thing altogether, rarer still by manyfold, when moons align.

It's like getting on the biggest rollercoaster you've ever been on. You're in the line-up and looking up at this towering thing, and there's a twist in your stomach. You're excited. It's bigger by a lot than any you've ever been on. And it's wooden. The biggest wooden rollercoaster in the world. The people in the line-up are saying it has a seventy-eight-degree drop. You're nervous and excited. And this guy comes around measuring people for maximum height, which I thought it was that you had to be *this tall* to get on the ride, but for *this* rollercoaster there's a maximum height for some reason, and this guy has a cigarette dangling out of the side of his mouth and he's measuring people with a stick that has a piece of metal sticking off the top that he's measuring with and he gives you the up and down, your head poking above the rest in the line-up, and he shuffles over and plunks the stick down next to you and you can feel your hair brush up against the piece of metal and the cigarette smoke seems to orbit the guy as if it'd be there whether he was smoking or not, and he grunts and jerks his head in one of those upward nods and he shuffles along again, the orbit of smoke following him, and the line-up makes another leap forward and you finally get to the front and you sit in the front row and you're waiting and then the gate and the *clickclickclickclickclick* up the hill and it's really steep and still *clickclickclickclickclick* and the cresting at the top and it's pulling hard right and your shoulder's yanked up against the side of the chair and you're hanging over nothing, quickly, and you remember the conversation about the seventy-eight-degree drop which now looks like a ninety-one-degree drop and you're hanging over this drop and you're about to start hurtling straight down toward the tiny distant land below, and it's all over but the crying now, and the rest of the train is pushing you forward and you drop and fall and, accelerating terminally, the wheels catch and simultaneous to the wheels catching you catch sight and now in slow motion watch the wooden crossbeam coming toward your forehead. And you think back to the guy with the smoke halo measuring for maximum height and you'd thought it was weird to measure for maximum height but obviously enormous wooden rollercoasters—this mammoth twisting labyrinthian craw of wood plunging chthonically down and inbetween the abysses on either side, of course it needs cross-beams to keep it steady. It still creaks, by the way, loudly. And you remember that the guy with the stick didn't exactly check to see how level the ground was and you don't want to be all uptight about the whole thing but for the fraction of space you weren't too tall by and this crossbeam coming at your forehead, in slow motion, while you're at terminal acceleration and you don't even know whose mercy you seek at this point as it whooshes over your ducking head and the car hits the bottom of the drop and swings up and your heart's at your throat and you're yanked a bank left turn and another beam whooshes over your head and you didn't have time to duck and your head is still intact and right at that moment, that moment when you're tingling everywhere, eyes wide, excited that you survived and excited for what's to come and this feeling of exhilarated peace surrounds you—at top speed—in that moment of that, whatever that is, well, I feel like that all the time when I'm with you, is what I told her.

She said *I'll see you tomorrow at midnight* and was gone.

My room was too small for what was going through it so I got in the car and picked up a package of cigarettes and drove up to a secluded peak and got out and looked out at the ocean under the full moon and got back in the car and rolled down my window and finished the dart, flicked it, and rolling up the window again noticed that through the glass I could see the moon's light refracted through the window into two beams shining outward like an orbit, like they were encircling the whole earth, and though I could only see a tiny fraction of the celestial halo in that moment I was quite sure the rest of it was certainly there in the sky, neither pointing nor directing, but embracing, swaddling me in its nighttime glow.

I drove home under the phosphorescent stars. I sat at the kitchen table and ate cream crackers and the last scraps of cheese out of the barren fridge and crawled into my bed and slept, dreaming of a distant imaginary land in which she wasn't married, and I woke up wanting to believe in possibilities.

She texted me in the morning anyway and we went for a drive along the coast without plan or destination. Beaches and lookouts and rocks and fog and graffiti and garbage. Having assured me she did not have a license and had only driven twice before in her life, I let her drive along the winding back road that connected the coast to civilization. We spent half the time on the shoulder and the other half laughing as the car bounced from pothole to pothole. Instead of taking the quick and easy back to the house I got her to turn right and asked her if she was okay to keep going but down a busier road and she nodded and so we went. Cars and trucks whizzed by and she kept ducking oncoming traffic, little swerves off to the right, slowing down for peripheral non-obstacles, anxiety the only thing in between us and a clear road in front, and the line of cars behind us grew and so I suggested we turn off at an upcoming side road, and she slowed a little, and turned a little, but not enough of either, and we drove straight toward the ditch and I looked at the ditch and it hit me that we were headed there and I yelled "Brake!" and I grabbed the wheel and yanked it right and she slammed the brakes and we skidded to a stop, the front bumper hanging over the edge.

Her eyes were wide and I kissed her again and again, and she apologized and I asked her not to and she kissed me and I asked her if she would keep driving because I trusted her and she trusted me that it was okay and we turned around and kept going down the winding road. I went to bed and slept, dreaming of waves and sand, and woke up rejecting the idea of possibilities.

Things just are.

She got depressed around Christmas. I just figured the cold was setting in, away from home for the holidays and all of that. Figured we could change it up and make it work. You can't keep the cold from seeping in around here, but you can make yourself so busy you don't have time to think about it. It was February by the time I realized that hadn't worked. I had been coming home late, keeping myself busy. And then one night in the middle of a snowstorm, in a wall of mute snow I came home and she ran out the door. Came back a few hours later with the better part of a half-case gone. The second time it happened I knew it was happening but I figured if I ran after her she'd know she could use it to get my attention. So I stayed home, kept the heat going, kept a light on, hoping she'd make it back. It's hard watching someone walk out the door, not knowing if they're going to live through the night.

It was probably around then that possibilities crept back in. That either she'd make it back or she wouldn't. The doctors were giving her pills, but she was spiralling faster than the pills were working. I came home to an empty prescription bottle on the counter, and she was passed out cold junk on the couch. I started shaking her frantically, needing her eyes to open and trying to remember how many pills had been in the bottle.

She woke up.

I realize it's been so long I can't even tell what love is anymore. I forgot that there are crossbeams. And when you're hurtling toward them you just have to believe you're not going to lose your head to it. She had been the one withstanding the crossbeams. I was the one who jumped out of the way.

In front of the computer I open a writing notebook, absent-mindedly clicking a retractable ballpoint pen. *Clickclickclickclickclick.*

Holes

Melissa Barbeau

WATER SLUICES DOWN the drains on the sides of the road. It is Saturday night and it is raining a thick, heavy, viscous rain. A river runs over the steps that lead down onto George Street. Boys fashion boats from empty cigarette packs and set them a sail on the muddy water, watching them tumble over the rapids and torrents, while girls in little dresses wait shivering, their hair clotted around them like seaweed.

Inside the bar the heat is tropical. Bodies are sweating as music pumps out of the speakers and the walls sweat too, they are wet to the touch. The room smells of animals. The door is propped open. A cool breeze slithers around our ankles like a snake but no one tries to escape. The music is hypnotic and so loud the room is vibrating and everyone is drunk and someone later telling the story will say people moved like one body but that isn't true. It is more like when you see something moving in a back alley and think there's an animal there, a cat or a rat, but really it's a thousand maggots separately squirming and fighting for their bite of rotten meat and it's only an illusion that they're moving in concert.

It is somewhere around the middle of the night and someone, a man, leans in and puts his mouth close to my ear and asks if I want a drink. All night he has eeled his way around the room, brushing up against a brunette with heavy bangs and a blonde with tippy heels that sway one way and then the other until she finally falls into a solid looking guy with armfuls of tattoos and the faintest suggestion of a long-repaired harelip. I say yes to the drink and we dance and he introduces me to his friends as if we've known each other for years, as if we know each other's last names, touching my hip to make sure I still exist alongside him. The blood beneath the spot he has touched spits and fizzes like champagne bubbles. He puts his hand on the small of my back and smiles at me over the rim of his glass and I cannot see his mouth but in the light that pulses from red to green to blue his eyes are dark and bottomless.

And then we are leaving the hot, slippery air of the bar for the warm, wet air of a springtime night. We run, holding hands, for the line of cabs at the end of the street, trying to avoid the stream of water and refuse, trying to avoid the deluges pouring from the roofs in waves. He throws open the door of a cab and we crawl in and the relative silence within the car envelops us. There is the spit and hiss of the dispatcher, pebbles of rain hit the roof, the wiper blades swish, but it is all wrapped in a gauzy layer of quiet. The driver is taciturn and after asking Where to? doesn't speak. He has a throat lozenge in his mouth and the air in the cab smells of menthol. It clicks against his teeth as he moves it around inside his mouth with his tongue.

The man and I sit in the backseat pressed leg to leg. His hand is moving up my thigh. His fingers are hard as if the flesh has fallen away and he is touching me with his bare bones. A subterranean rumbling fills my ears. It floods the car, a noise like the sound of engines starting when you are standing on the deck of the ferry, a noise that starts in the soles of your feet and moves its way upward through your body.

The car crawls up New Gower past the churchyards with their flocks of prostitutes leaning against the fences like sodden sparrows. We snake our way through the labyrinth that is Rawlins Cross with its riddle of one ways and yields and do not turn rights. We come up along Bannerman Park. There is a house on the corner with a little hexagonal window and in the window is the face of a person, a bust, and sometimes the face looks in at the interior of the house and sometimes she sits in profile but today she is looking out as we pass, watching us drive by in the taxi. The Needs Convenience is ablaze with light and then, again, the noise.

The noise is guttural and low. The cab begins to shake. A thousand dishes clatter. Panes of glass begin to fall from the buildings lining the street, shattering like melting icicles in a spring thaw. There is the sharp crack of branches snapping from ancient trees. The man grabs at my hand. In the cab there is still an envelope of silence and no one says anything, no one curses or prays or exclaims and when the earth stops trembling he opens the door and the silence that has been contained inside the vehicle floods out. He pulls me onto the road and the whole world is quiet, the calm thick. The rain has stopped.

A hole has opened in the pavement in front of the cab. The driver has come out also and is gazing into it. A car has fallen in and a truck. A big piece of the sidewalk is missing and the porch on the house in the corner is still attached but barely. It is leaning. It is literally holding on by the nails. I wonder if the face in the window still has her nose, her ears. The man grabs at me and we leave the cab behind and begin to walk across the park. There are holes everywhere, holes with no bottoms, in the ground but also in the skyline, places where there had been trees but now there are not. A tree lies across a hole like a bridge. A telephone pole has been uprooted, the wires have come loose. There is the sound of electricity snapping and a tree catches on fire, flames shooting skywards.

We stop next to the gazebo. The roof has caved in. There is a pop and the lights go out and there is the second of space, like the second between throwing a coin and it hitting the bottom of a wishing well and the man is suddenly, frantically kissing me, his hands like manic crabs pinching at the buttons of my shirt, the hem of my skirt, my hair. His lips cover mine. I am suffocating. He fills my mouth with his tongue. I try to remove his pinchers, pluck at his arms. He is strong. Once, in the summer, I had taken my niece to see the seals at the Marine Lab in Logy Bay and there had been a touch tank filled with sea creatures: crabs and sea anemones with undulating tentacles and clams that opened and shut their mouths and sea cucumbers that were leathery and slippery at the same time and heavy with sea water and that is what his tongue feels like as it touches my teeth and I bite it and the crabs let go and I run. It is dark and I run and he is right behind me running in the dark with the holes and then there is a tree root reaching out like a finger and I trip and fall onto my side and he is behind me and also trips but instead falls forward and then he is hanging on. He has caught himself on the root and he is dangling and I crawl over to look and I cannot see the bottom. The pit is at the edge of a perfectly intact flowerbed. There is a row of golden marigolds and another of pansies. The soil I am kneeling in is wet and black. Hard little twigs that have snapped off their branches press into the flesh of my hands.

He looks up at me with his eyes that are black holes and his mouth with its tongue like a sea creature starts to make words but I stand and smash down on his fingers with the heel of my boot again and again and I don't hear him say anything, not one single word, and then he is gone.

I hear sirens in the distance. The park smells of fresh dirt, of spring. The wind begins to blow, a low, keening howl. I pull my sweater tight around me and begin the long walk home.

23 Things I Hate in No Particular Order

Gary Newhook

I'M PISSED OFF and I'm drunk, so I'm good and uninhibited now. I know you would not approve, Dr. Carlson, but this was the only way the letter was going to happen. I will probably feel like a dope when you make me read this at the next meeting. Yes, I am breaking the fourth wall here, writing non-fiction is not my strong suit (Ha ha).

First, I will tell you about my childhood.

I think I was a pretty normal kid. I drew little pictures, I played Nintendo with my older brother, Clarke, and my room was caked in Transformers. I had Transformers wallpaper, a Transformers bedspread, and the two-foot tall Optimus Prime that turned into a transport truck. I would draw pictures of Transformers in an exercise book on the table in the corner of my room, and I'd write little stories to go with the pictures.

My dad bought the exercise books off me for a dollar apiece as I finished each one. I think this is because my mother told him they should encourage my talent. She always read these articles in *Reader's Digest* and other magazines about raising your child with the self-esteem they would need to survive the digital age. She really believed all that stuff.

We lived on a farm on Pork Chop Hill. It wasn't really an active farm in my lifetime; we just called it the farm. My great-grandfather raised pigs there, and then my grandfather raised pigs there, then my father decided he would be a veterinarian instead of raising pigs. What we called the farm when I was growing up was just a big grassy field behind our house.

The earliest thing I can remember is sitting in my room, colouring. I don't remember what I was colouring, but that probably isn't important.

My mother shouted, "Clarence! Look out your window!"

When I looked out the window, my dad was driving around on the farm in a baby-blue minivan. He waved and the long blades of grass tickled the chassis. We all piled in the van and I remember the buttons on the tape deck. They looked like big blocks of dark chocolate that made a loud thunk when you pushed them.

It was the first new vehicle my father ever owned. That night, he took us to the Dairy Queen on Topsail Road.

That should be enough to set things up, really. A fairly typical childhood for someone growing up right outside St. John's. Now, for the other thing you asked me to write about, here is a list of things that makes me angry when I think about them. These are in no particular order:

1) Paying taxes to the municipal government. I feel like no matter how high taxes get, no matter how far they push the mill rate up, town services don't get any better. Why, why, why is my road always last to get plowed in winter? Most of the men on the snow clearing crew are these big bubbas with grade-eight educations who don't know what they're doing.

2) People who don't come to the animal shelter for their pets. On the last Thursday of every month, the local SPCA rounded up all the unclaimed animals and brought them to my father to be put down. On those days, he picked up a flask of Golden Wedding on the way home from work. He sat in the big recliner by the living-room window and stared out at the farm. The longer he sat there, the more Golden Wedding he put in the glass relative to the amount of water.

One evening he called me over and said, "Clarence, we are never getting a dog."

I asked why.

He said, "Because I should have been a pig farmer."

3) The hacks at *South Coast Post Literary Magazine* in South Africa. They rejected my short story "Island" on the basis of not

publishing science fiction. How stupid is that? They just excluded an entire genre of writing! Heaven forbid people broaden their horizons.

4) While I'm on the subject of "Island," thinking about Jack Chipman makes me angry. When we were in high school, the English teachers held a short-story contest. That's when I wrote the first draft of "Island." It was the first thing I wrote since I sold my father Transformers picture books for a dollar. Fucking Jack Chipman wrote a story about coming out of the closet. Guess who won?

I am sick of people crossing politics with art. Your fiction, or any art, should not be a biography about how your cousin touched you and that led to your realization you were gay because you sort of liked it. The teacher who judged the contest was Miss Williams, a pumpkinesque woman who always wanted to seem like she was on the bleeding edge of progressiveness. She sat me down and explained that Chipman's story was more riveting.

5) Clarke always got to be Mario in *Mario Bros. 3*.

6) A community group successfully lobbied to get my hometown renamed. They said Pork Chop Hill was too morbid a name for a town full of young families. But Pork Chop Hill has a ton of history. There were a bunch of pig farms up there including my grandfather's. It's called Heaven's Acres now. I hardly go up there anymore.

7) Our next-door neighbour, Missus Evens, grew potatoes on the big hill behind her house. She filled empty Eversweet Margarine tubs with beer and put them all over the hill to keep slugs out of the potatoes. The smell of the beer drew the slugs toward the butter tubs, and then they'd fall in and drown.

When I was eleven and Clarke was twelve, we snuck into her potato garden and drank all the beer. It was early August, so the potato plants were two or three feet tall. We crawled between them on all fours, exploring our own miniature jungle. Most of the butter tubs had limp, white slug corpses in them. The beer was flat and watery and I was pretty drunk after two or three tubs. Clarke poked his head through the potato plants, and shouted "Ogga booga!" like a jungle man and I laughed until my stomach hurt.

The accelerated growth of Pork Chop Hill took care of Missus Evens' potato garden. Two years later, she sold her land to a developer and moved to an old folks' home in St. John's. I watched them chip away at the potato garden, as it gave way to a subdivision full of prefabricated shitboxes. It's been so long since I've seen it, when I close my eyes, I can barely picture the rows of potato blossoms anymore. Me and Clarke had so much fun up there.

8) It's years later and they're building another subdivision where the farm used to be. The same place my poor old dad drove around in his new van, the same place I buried my hamster in a

little cardboard casket and the same place me and Clarke used to play soccer.

Sometimes I go up there and watch them working on the lots. If I sit there for too long, I just get angrier and angrier, so here's what I do: I put a few mints in my mouth and let them sit on my tongue. Once they dissolve on their own, I know it's time to leave.

Lot 15 on Spring Hill Road is around where my hamster should have been buried. When they were working on the lot, I asked a man on a backhoe if he had dug up a hamster in a little cardboard casket. He said no, they had not dug up any hamsters that day. The lot is covered in grey compacted stone now, so I guess when they were trucking off the old topsoil, they trucked off my hamster as well.

9) *Collards and Things*—a farming journal in Iowa that prints a short story in the back every month. They rejected "Island" because they found the premise too farfetched. The plot goes something like this: Global warming accelerates as humanity enters the 2100s, the ice caps melt, and the last people are living on an island in the Pacific, the only piece of dry land left on the planet as far as they know. The ocean has become so polluted and acidic they can't leave the island, so they have to learn to get along as their food supply dwindles. A situation ripe for drama. It writes itself, really.

10) The road they put behind our house when I was twelve. Dad

got a letter from the town that said they were expropriating a portion of his land to put in a new road. It said he would be given fair market value for the land, and it explained that this sort of action was sometimes required in a growing town. My mother balled up the letter and threw it in the woodstove, but the road still got built anyway.

The road was ten feet away from the back door. My brother and I spent that summer sitting on the back step, popsicles in hand, watching the road crew eat away a sliver of the big field that was always there. After that, we had one tenth of an acre of land on one side of the road, and nearly twelve acres on the other.

Mom and dad fell into a bit of a routine following that. Every Friday they walked down to the store with the liquor outlet and my mother bought a half-dozen radio bingo tickets and my father bought a twenty-sixer of Golden Wedding. Sometimes he watched her play bingo, but most times he stared out the window at the blackened gulf between our house and the farm. When a set of headlights went up the road he said, "Someone's driving on the farm." My mother wouldn't look up from her bingo cards.

11) All the flyers the government sends me in the mail. How much does it cost to mail all that shit? People are crying for new hospitals and schools and road work. The government comes out and says they don't have the money to pay for any of it, but then they send me a four-colour brochure in the mail every time someone in the Confederation Building takes a shit.

12) This girl from high school, Amy. I was out drinking with some people from school. I didn't drink much back then, but it was the 24th of May weekend, and everyone drinks on the 24th of May weekend. We were camping in this big field up behind town. It used to be a sod farm, but by that point it was an island of grass in a sea of trees. You can see why it was a popular teenage drinking spot.

The fire was going really good and everyone was drinking beer, and I was way too drunk, way too early. I sat on a cooler by the fire and this Amy girl, this blonde with glasses and a tank top that showed off just a little cleavage said, "I have nowhere to sleep tonight."

Without thinking, I said, "I'm in a three-man tent by myself."

She didn't look at me. She didn't say yes or no or thanks. She just said, "OK."

I crawled in the tent and passed out on top of my sleeping bag. The sound of the tent door unzipping woke me up. I couldn't focus very well, because I was still really wasted, but I could make out Amy crawling in. She lay down next to me and stared at me, and I was staring back, and I kissed her. Really quick. Just a quick peck on the lips. Then she didn't react and everything was really still and quiet for a long time. Then she kissed me back. The next thing I remember she was on top of me and our pants were down around our ankles. I was trying to keep a good rhythm with my hips, but I was terrible at it and my ears were pounding and the top of the tenting was throbbing in and out to the beat of the pounding in my ears and it was making me sick so I closed my eyes and that's the last thing I remember.

That week in school, Amy wouldn't talk to me. We probably didn't say two words to each other after that. It does make me mad, in a weird way, when I think about it.

The field is probably a subdivision now. I haven't been up there since then.

13) Every time I buy seeds and plant them, they never grow.

14) One Friday night, Clarke and I were watching *The Simpsons* on channel twenty-six. Mom and Dad left to head down to the store like they always did.

John Molson walked into the living room. His last name wasn't really Molson, I don't think. Everyone called him John Molson because he was always on the beer. A forty-year bender. I don't know his real last name. His hair and beard were white. He always reminded me of a wizard from a fantasy story. John Molson the perpetually drunk.

My brother said, "Why are you here, John?"

John Molson had this faraway look in his eyes. He walked over to the kitchen table and sat down. He didn't say anything. He just sat and stared at the wall.

The reek of stale beer permeated the house.

I leaned in toward Clark: "Should we throw him out?"

We figured John Molson got too drunk and got lost.

Then John Molson started to cry. Face in his hands, full-on bawling. Here we were, watching TV and this drunk man just comes in our kitchen and starts to cry. It was really fucked up. He lifted his head and looked at us, "Boys, phone the police. I just ran over your parents."

15) Why can't we figure out a mixture of paint that will stay on the road for an entire winter? I don't know if I'm supposed to turn or go straight.

16) The *Shaggy Summit Literary Magazine* out of Canmore, Alberta. They said that while they did like the idea of the last remnants of humanity being stranded on an island together, not entirely sure if they are the only ones left, they found the protagonist's story arc uncompelling. The main character loses his family in the flood, and they thought that was something the reader should see unfold within the story. What if he is trying to save his family so we can really cheer for him? The editor finished with, and I quote, "We want to see a character whose whole world disintegrates before our very eyes, not one whose life is already in shambles."

17) I was eighteen, and Clarke was nineteen, when John Molson killed our parents, so we were allowed to stay in the house. Clarke was studying to become an electrician at CONA. He did his apprenticeship at South East Electrical in Bay Bulls.

They mostly did electrical work on long liners. It was a weird niche, but they were always busy. When he finished his apprenticeship, he went ahead and got his journeyman. I worked at the bakery during this time period.

Clarke sat me down at the kitchen table one evening and told me he was moving to Alberta to make some real money. I told him I understood, but honestly, it does make me pretty mad when I think about it even now. Here was my brother, my best friend in the entire world, sitting at the same place at the table John Molson sat, telling me he was leaving.

When he went to bed that night, I crossed the street to the farm. I looked at the road between the farm and our house, my house now, and then I looked up at the fledging subdivision in Missus Evens' former potato garden, and I felt so incredibly frustrated I wanted to hit something. I punched the ground. Then I stood up and stomped on the ground. Then I shouted at our house, "How could you leave me stuck here?"

I don't know if Clarke heard me that night. It's never come up.

18) I can't go in anyone's house nowadays without getting assaulted by the smell of Febreze.

19) Thinking about last winter makes me pretty angry. I was sitting in the kitchen, this was around mid-January, and the whole house shook. I mean, things fell off the counter and everything.

My first thought was an earthquake at sea or something like that. I heard someone cursing downstairs. I went down there, and this big yellow salt truck with the plow on the front had driven into the side of the house, tearing out an entire downstairs wall. The driver was pacing back and forth, swearing. He said there wasn't enough salt on the road and his truck skidded on the ice.

20) This is related: I'm mad as hell I had to sell the farm. The town refused to pay for the damage to my house, and the insurance company wouldn't help me rebuild. They both cited town bylaw 32(a): "No home shall be located within fifteen feet of a public roadway." They said this absolved them of all blame. If I had been following town bylaws, this wouldn't have happened. I didn't take it to court. I was too tired. I called my brother in Alberta and we sold the house and the farm to a developer and I bought a two-bedroom condo in St. John's with my share.

21) People should not let their cats outside. Cats that are kept indoors tend to live longer and have a decreased chance of contracting feline AIDS. They are also harmful to the local ecosystem.

22) There is an overpass between St. John's and Pork Chop Hill, or Heaven's Acres or whatever the hell it is now. In early March, I stood up there with a big cinder block, and I waited. The town depot is near the overpass, so all the snow clearing equipment drives under it at the end of the shift.

I waited for Salt Truck 004, the salt truck that ran into my house. When it drove under the overpass, I threw the cinderblock through the windshield. Salt Truck 004 swerved to the side and ran head-on into the overpass. The driver I met in my basement got all busted up. The whole thing was satisfying, like when you crack your knuckles.

They gave me probation and sentenced me to anger management at the Waterford once a week until I was deemed fit to stop. I think I'm fit to stop now, so I'm pretty mad at getting forced to waste my time.

23) I started drinking and got all uninhibited on account of my latest rejection. I sent the latest version of "Island" into a short-story contest the government was holding. The judge's biggest complaint was about the ending.

See, in "Island" the water in the Pacific Ocean is so acidic it starts to dissolve the island everyone is living on. The island gets smaller and smaller, and one by one, everyone falls in and dies until the main character is left standing on a rock in the Pacific all by himself. We don't know what happens, it's meant to be open-ended.

The judge thought the protagonist should just surrender and let himself fall into the ocean. He is the last person alive, what's left for him to live for? Everything he's ever known and loved has ceased to exist.

Benched

Susan Sinnott

THE CROWD WAS lifting off its feet, shouting. The horn gave a blast and the organ played one of those special hockey tunes—sounds you only hear in rinks. Da da da daa, da daaaa. The P.A. announced the goal, "And an assist by Gus Sheppard."

And all the Sheppards went crazy, cheering fit to burst and Hutch was jumping up and down with them, fizzing with energy, giving off sparks. One of their own was down there on the ice and people were yelling his name. The roar bounced off the walls and circled and crashed over them like breakers.

It was different watching a game on television with replays from every angle so you could see just who did what. Hutch saw Gus deking two players in a row and making a pass across the goal, but he couldn't see the winger flick it in—just saw the puck hit the back of the net as the red light flashed. They put it all together afterwards, on the bus.

Dad always said you saw more of the game on TV. He hadn't come. But at the game itself you were right in it—felt the vibrations up through your bones, the noise exploding in your head. You smelled winter melting off people's jackets, wet wool, dust from old concrete and hot dogs and aftershave. You were part of the crowd when it roared to its feet at that perfect moment.

It had been a rush to get ready. Not that Hutch did much, outside of rooting about in cupboards looking for the old Newfoundland flag, until his mom growled about the mess. Mr. and Mrs. Sheppard did all the work: the block of tickets at the stadium in St. John's, transport from Mariners Cove. There were too many people for one bus so they joined up with the crowd from over Gander way, which was where the Sheppard cousin came from, the one who was playing. He'd been called up from the East Coast League to play a game in the American League, with the Maple Leafs' farm team.

The youngest Sheppards got to make the banner: Jenny and Jack—Go Gus Go in blue letters on white. Looked great. Jenny was good at that stuff. And here they were, jumping up and down next to him, and Eugene and the rest bouncing on Hutch's other side, and all that carroty Sheppard hair sticking out under blue Leafs caps, and Gus on the ice with his big orange beard.

The first period was a bit slow but it picked up in the second with a goal each and a whole bunch of shots on net and a couple of nice little fights. Then Gus got that assist with three minutes to go and it was a big deal because they won three to two in overtime.

They came out of the stadium around eleven into a mix of snow, sleet, and freezing rain.

"St. John's," said Eugene. "Even the weather doesn't know its ass from a hole in the ground."

No use griping about the weather. Ignore it. But if you're on the eastern edge of everything with your face in the North Atlantic and a four hour drive after the game, you can never ignore the weather.

The first bus was pulling out as Hutch wandered across the car park with the Sheppards. After they'd banged on the side of the bus a bit and shouted goodbye and caused a nice bit of havoc, they piled into the second one. They took over the back three rows.

There were replays everywhere. Definitely high sticking. Should have… Did you see? Jack dug a bologna sandwich out of his back pack, a bit squashed. He gave Hutch half and they shared Hutch's Cheesies. Hutch said Jack's hands matched his hair and Jack yelled, "Redhead Joke," and rubbed his cheesy hands into Hutch's face. Eugene leaned over the top of the seat from behind and grabbed Hutch's baseball cap, scrobbed his hair and rammed the cap back down on Hutch's head, laughing that big boom of a laugh that set off everyone around. There were chuckles all down the aisle, people craning round to scc, murmurs of, "Oh, Eugene," and "There goes Eugene." It was comfortable tucked away inside the bus, friendly. Black as your heart outside.

After an hour or two there was a change of topic here and there, to local stuff and plans for next week. Fathers leaned back and closed eyes. Mr. Sheppard was snoring in the row in front and Jack's mom leaned across the aisle to chat to her sister. Eugene and the guys were singing some old Beatles songs in back with Jenny adding top notes in a jokey kind of soprano. Hutch joined in with "Love, love me do," and turned round and grinned at her.

Jack went up front for a minute. Hutch turned more into the corner, leaned his head against the window and shoved the hood of his jacket between him and the glass to cut down the chill. He stretched his legs out diagonally, feet under the seat in front on Jack's side. They stretched a long way. He'd grown a nice bit this last year. He shifted about, trying to untangle his foot from the straps of Jack's backpack, closed his eyes. Then he dropped. The bus dropped, tilted, went black.

Twelve holes across. Twelve holes the other way. 144 holes each tile. Ten tiles over to the wall makes 1440. Seven tiles to the fluorescent light makes—eight, carry two—1,008 holes. A woman was looking down at him, her face coming, going, coming. It steadied. Looked like Mom. No she didn't but she had the same stop-messing-around-and-listen face.

"Glad you're awake, Hutch."

A nurse. It took a while for the information to sink in—like a dry sponge that floats on the water for a bit before it starts getting wet. An accident. The bus…Bus? Gone off the road on a bend. Bad visibility. Ice build-up. Crashed rear end first down a bank. Holy shit. He tried to get his tongue to work, to ask questions.

He had the worst of the injuries: both legs broken, some ribs. But a lot of folks had broken bones, concussions, soft tissue injuries—whatever they were—a punctured lung from a fractured rib, a small heart attack. Didn't know they came in sizes.

He started to remember more, singing and eating Cheesies, nothing about the crash. He asked where everyone was. Mom said folks hurt the least were taken to hospital in Gander and Clarenville, but they'd brought Hutch straight to town. What about Jack?

"A minor concussion and a broken arm. Gone to Gander."

"And Jenny and Eugene?"

Mom paused. "Not sure where they were taken," she said. "Weren't brought into St John's."

His parents kept getting into a huddle with whatever nurse walked in the door, muttering so he couldn't hear. "Just checking," they said when he asked. "Just making sure everything's being done."

There was a meeting.

They wheeled his bed with all those tubes and stuff into this tiny space off the Intensive Care Unit and the walls swung round as the bed moved and kept on swinging when it stopped. They were slow and careful but something bumped and he felt the bump go all through him. Felt like he'd jumped down off a wall onto concrete. Tried to move a bit, to ease his legs, but it only made it worse.

Mom and Dad came in. Smiled at him but their eyes were scary. There was a tall guy in a white coat with a hawk face and bushy old-man eyebrows, and a younger doc wearing a name tag, somebody MacPherson, and the nurse who was around all the time with the sing-song voice. Then a grey-head with brown folders under her arm and glasses that kept sliding down. Never seen her before. The nurse introduced everybody. Head nurse. Hawk Face was the orthopaedic guy and his name had *ov* and *evsky* in it like hockey names all run together. That nurse's voice was nice but distracting—he kept listening to the voice not the words. Not from round here. Welsh, she told him afterwards. The other woman was a social worker.

The Head Nurse looked at his mom and dad and him, each in turn, and talked about the accident and his injuries. Chatty.

Said something about his rib cage, something thoracic crushed. Crushed didn't sound good. He couldn't get too excited though because it all sounded so far away, nothing to do with him. Stable spine. Discs, nerve roots…pressure. Inflammation. Swelling going down nicely. Wait and see. Lost a lot of blood, under control, lucky the paramedics got to him when they did. God.

"And I'll let Dr. …evsky explain about the legs."

He looked straight at Hutch. Nice he was talking to him but hard to be stared at like that. Just him. That guy standing and him stuck flat on his back. Made him feel like something in Science with a pin through it. What was he saying? The right leg had been sorted out but the left leg: "Bone fragments…tissue loss…vascular surgeon…" A whoosh of fear scorched through Hutch, white hot. "Limb salvage." Like a frigging ship wreck. Holy crap. "Best we can hope for." Not. Minimal. Unable. None. Eventually. "Best outcome, the most functional outcome, would be to remove the severely damaged leg below the knee and—"

"No. No!" Hutch was yelling in spite of his stitches. "No way you're cutting off my leg. Never."

Dad said My Boy, and Mom said Hutch, Hutch, and the doc kept on explaining and Hutch kept on yelling. Didn't care about the risk and all the surgeries, didn't care how good prosthetics were these days. He wanted his own leg. It was his fucking *leg*. He heard the doc saying, "Think about it and we'll talk later."

But he wasn't changing his mind. No way.

They moved him into a general ward. There were people in the other beds but he couldn't see them: a wall one side and screens on the other and him down flat. Dr. MacPherson was around a bit, the resident. Said he'd been to Mariners Cove once, paddled in with a group from university back when he was an undergrad.

"In sea kayaks?" Hutch was interested then and told the doc maybe he was with the group Dad saw. "Dad had a good look at a bunch of kayaks that visited and took a paddle in one and then built one himself. Still have it. Called *May* after my mom."

He said how the Parsons had always built their own boats for the inshore fishery but there was no market for them now, so Dad turned to kayaks instead. Sold about fifty. Hutch even told him about his own kayak that he'd built by himself, because he seemed an okay guy. But he went right on refusing an amputation. And everyone had a go at him: Dr. MacPherson, the family, the nurses—the frigging mail man was probably on his way.

Dad said he was thinking with his gut not his head and Mom said, "They're treating you like an adult, Hutch, giving you a choice."

"What choice? When I choose everyone yells at me, tells me I'm wrong."

Mom came nearer the bed, loomed over him. "Children your age usually go to the children's hospital. You only ended up here because the ICU was full or something. But you're still a child—"

"I'm not a frigging child." The roar made his ribs stab and he broke off. Dad shifted in his chair, told him to watch his tongue, and Mom glared at Dad for a change.

"I know it's hard, Hutch." There were tears in her eyes. "But you have to look facts in the face. You will walk better, do everything better, look better, have less side effects, *if* you have an amputation."

Hutch clamped his teeth together to keep his thoughts in, to keep himself from shaking. His heart was pounding like he'd just run up a hill. As if. Mom put her hand on his, gave it a little squeeze, moved away before he had time to fling it off. "We'll be back tomorrow. If you want us."

He tried to yell that he didn't, but he couldn't breathe, couldn't speak.

Dad stood up, chewing his lip. "We want what's best for you," he said after a bit. "You know that." He nodded down at Hutch, head poked forwards. "If it was someone else in this spot what would you tell them?" Then they were gone.

Hutch closed his eyes. Now he was alone, except for being picked at by some nurse or other, and corpse-man next to him with the beige screens round who he still hadn't seen, and the beeps and buzzers, the smells, the trolleys rattling, the loudspeaker calling for Dr. Murphy for the thousandth time. He'd never minded being alone. Always plenty to do, places to go. This was different. Felt like he wanted to hide and someone had moved the trees.

Everything was sliding away, out of control. Stuff was being done *to* him all the time, things he'd always done himself, taken for granted, even being washed, for God's sake. He'd tried to grab the facecloth out of the aide's hand, twisted his rib cage and given himself a real jolt.

Without the amputation he'd have one leg way shorter, might need more surgeries, might end up with the leg off anyway if things didn't work, maybe in and out of hospital for years. With an amputation and a prosthesis he could be functional in months and look almost normal. Get on with life. Or so they said.

But an amputation was so—forever.

He'd miss a hunk of school either way. And this was grade twelve. It mattered this time. He asked Dr. MacPherson when he'd be able to play hockey and the guy didn't look straight at him like he usually did and said something about early days. Well, doctors didn't know everything. God, he and Jack had really been working at it. The coach put them on the ice together because they were a good combination, Jack for speed and Hutch for power.

Power. He had no power now, over anything. Well, he could fill out that menu card and choose his breakfast. Yeah right. Prunes or grapefruit. The only real choice he had now was about the leg, and he wanted to tell them all to shove off. Functional much quicker. Get on with life.

A nurse said how it was lucky he was so fit and muscular and Hutch checked out his arms, noticed how flabby his biceps had gone, how they'd shrunk. That nurse didn't know what muscular was. His shoulders had gone away to nothing, his big kayaking shoulders. Plain vanished. Months to build them up and they were gone in a week. He couldn't believe it, kept checking. Gone.

Dr. MacPherson wanted to see that leg. Asked if Hutch had seen it yet. Said it was time. If he couldn't see lying down they'd find a mirror. The nurse was ages coming up with a mirror. Don't let her find one. Don't let her. The doc opened up the splint or whatever that was and all that padding. "Look at it, Hutch."

Fuck. Holy fuck.

The aide was bellowing in his ear. "Never ate your lunch, b'y."

Hutch looked at him, blank, and buddy lifted the cover off a plate near Hutch's nose. "Liver," he said. It looked like a piece of bark curled up at the edges with a mushy scoop of mashed potatoes and some dead carrots.

"Not hungry," Hutch said. "Thanks." He hadn't even noticed the food being brought and there was that little plastic thing the pills came in so the nurse had been round too. "When'll Dr. MacPherson be back?" It was an hour or so before the resident came.

"If I don't have the amputation, what would you have to do

to turn that—" he jabbed his chin towards the splint, "into a leg?"

The doc stood looking down at Hutch, said he needed pictures to explain. He came back later with this big book that looked like a school atlas—*Grant's Atlas of Anatomy*. He leaned it on the table, tilting it so Hutch could see. "This is what the lower leg looks like inside, the layers. See these bones, joints, these muscles..."

"So that's like a lever," said Hutch, after a bit.

The doc nodded. "Exactly."

"And the fulcrum should be down there but on my leg it's gone." He waited for the nod. "And you'd need to glue all those bits together before it could work again?" Yes. "And it wouldn't work anyway because the wiring's gone?" More nods. Hutch stared at the diagrams, flicked a page. "You do plumbing too?"

Dr. MacPherson smiled a little slow smile. Waited.

Hutch's throat closed up and his mouth felt like wrinkled cardboard. He'd have to change stuff kayaking. It meant letting go of hockey and hiking, even chasing a ball around the schoolyard. He'd walk like an old man. And girls. God, don't think about girls. Jenny. He could hear his mom. Nice girls won't care. Yes. But. He tried to speak but had to clear his throat and start again. He took a tight breath and forced the words out so they came out in a bellow, like when his voice was breaking.

"Better take it off then."

Mom and Dad were smiling when they came back, hugged him, said they were proud of him. He'd just needed time to think it through.

"So now you can stop whispering to all the nurses." Hutch's grin felt a bit stiff.

And they both stood there like lumps and that scary look was back in their eyes.

"What?" He looked from one to the other. "What?" Nobody spoke. "Tell me."

"Eugene and Jenny," Mom said. Stopped. "The back of the bus." She was whispering. "It went through the ice into a pond."

Dad put his arm round her. "They were killed, Hutch. They're gone."

Hutch lay there. The facts seeped into the edges of him but his insides had frozen solid. Eugene and Jenny? Couldn't be. He just lay there. Now and then something tiny would float up: Jenny splashing him with her paddle, Eugene's big front teeth. After a while he turned his head away, pulled the sheet up over his face.

Like Jewels

Jamie Fitzpatrick

I WAITED TILL a couple of weeks after the funeral. After they cleared away the wreck and it wasn't in the papers anymore. That's when I went out to the highway with my flashlight and tape measure.

Mother had given up going to bed altogether. She'd be on the couch every night with the TV up on bust. Never watched anything. Just click-click-click all night long. Come around eleven o'clock one night I sat on the basement stairs and waited. When the channels stopped changing and I could hear it was just the one show with the ads and all, that's when I knew she was out. The glasses all twisted on her face and the clicker gone down in the cushions.

Out the back door then. Kicked a plank out of Foley's fence—it only took one good boot—squeezed through there and I was down the street in no time. Took the shortcut behind Comfort Inn and started up the highway. Sweating through my shirt. Another hot night with no wind at all and the nippers were at me. Flies were bad that year.

There were two skid marks. Just past the Esso station, where the road turns for the bridge. They started in the right lane and went across to the other shoulder. One was thick and curved like a big eyebrow. The other was thin and you could read the tread pattern in it, the way it pulled sideways. There was no keeping that car on the road. I'd say he hardly got his foot on the brake, it happened that quick. I bent down and dug my nails into the thick one. It was cool and wet from the midnight dew. My nails came out all black. There was the smell of rubber from the sun baking it every day.

Nobody could tell Margaret what to do. She wouldn't do the decent thing and sneak away with Nate Cumby. Had to make a show of herself, out driving around with him. Everyone knew Nate and his blue Camaro with the Canadian Club stickers up the side of the windshield. Everyone saw Margaret next to him. They knew her husband was left home with baby Jeremy. Margaret should have been home and they should have been a family. What kind of girl doesn't want her baby? There was nothing but shame in it. I tried not to take much notice. I was seventeen years old and nothing my big sister did ever made sense to me. So what odds. But it must have been bad for mother.

The bartender at the Airport Club said they were there most of the afternoon, playing pool. Bold as brass. Nate Cumby must have been pleased with himself, out shooting pool with another man's wife. Not even trying to hide it. Buddy who worked at the Esso station said he was pumping gas when the Camaro flew by. Doing a hell of a clip, he said. Suppertime on a Tuesday, and summer nearly over. Hardly another car on the road.

It was the baby drove Margaret to it. She wasn't ready for a baby, especially a baby that was sick right from the start. At first they thought Jeremy wouldn't live more than a few days. Maybe it would have been better for everyone if he didn't, with all the trouble after. When he was born they had to keep track of every breath, every heartbeat. Margaret and her husband wrote it all down in a book, and some days she would leave the hospital and bring the book over to show mother. There were days when it seemed like he was stronger, and days when it seemed like he might not hang on at all. But by Christmas they were able to take him home. So everything should have been better after that. But Margaret couldn't take it. It was like the baby made her sick too, and he could manage with it but she couldn't.

It was bad. Closed casket. People came to the house with cakes and pea soup and Mass cards. I remember a big casserole, must have had three or four pounds of hamburger in it. They all came to the funeral and the next day they went back to their lives like it was nothing to them. They buried Nate somewhere else. He was from Plate Cove, I believe.

That was my first summer working construction. Pellerin was a real bastard, had me on the run every day. But I was proud of that job. Never left the house without my tape measure. So when I was out there on the highway I felt for it on my belt and got down on my knees. There was no moon, but the big sign was lit up over the Esso station. I got the tape out and took the measure of the skid marks. The big one was nearly three times as wide, and had the steeper curve. The thin one had little gaps in it. Each gap bigger than the last by an eighth or quarter inch, and then half an inch, and then the better part of three inches. The car trying to get airborne, right before she flipped. Nate with a big grin on his face and a hairy elbow hanging out the window. Margaret with the bottle between her legs. I turned my flashlight to the gully, where the grass was all flat and dead, with bits of the windshield sparkling in it, like jewels.

Jeremy never had much to do with us after that. They brought him around a couple of times when he was a baby. Then they stopped coming, and mother just let it be. She hardly left the house anymore. Still on the couch every night with the TV.

It might have been different if Jeremy was a regular boy. But he was never well, and they used to take him away to the doctors on the mainland. In the summers he'd be home. One year, he must have been seven or eight years old, and I'd see him and his father every day out on Bennett Drive. Pellerin had us down there doing the new bungalows and split-levels. It was shoddy work too, the way he was rushing us along. And they'd be coming down the sidewalk. Jeremy putting one foot in front of the other. Fighting it, because the feet didn't want to go and he had to force them. His father holding his arm and nudging him along.

After that they sent him to a special school somewhere, and you would always see his picture in the paper, winning a prize for math or science or something. His body was still all wrong. You could see it in the pictures, the way his shoulder lifted up to one of his ears. But you could see Margaret in him, too. Even when he smiled he had a hard face on him, like you just said something. Like he was ready to fight. It was Margaret's look.

I couldn't take living with mother anymore, so I went to Toronto. I think she wanted the house to herself anyway. Said she'd pay my board until I got a job up there. I was over thirty years old by then. But it wasn't easy, I tell you. Picked up a few cash jobs doing carpentry, tried to get on with the recycling depot. Then mother stopped paying the board and when I called her up she said, "You always wanted to be special and you were never anything special, believe me." So that was it. Out on the street. It was bad for a while, until I got on with the road crew, painting lines every summer. Finally got myself straightened out.

Never talked to mother for years, five or six years at least. She found me, I don't know how. Called a few times. But I never called back. Not until the day I was on a job site and went into the porta-potty and tried to pee. Blood came out. Nearly black, it was that dark coming out of me. I started sweating and shaking. One of the boys dropped me at the hospital and they put me in ICU. First they put a catheter in right down below, and then I had the IV. They stuck so many tubes in me I thought I'd never come out of it.

At the end of the week they said I could go. I called mother and said I'm coming home out of it. Mother bought the plane ticket because I couldn't ride the bus, the state I was in. She had to go off her medication to pay for it. She keeps a diary of her medication, and she showed it to me. Nine weeks she couldn't afford it because she paid for my ticket. Says she's never been the same since, after the nine weeks and everything else I put her through, and Dr. Snow says she'll never be the same again.

She says it nearly killed her when I left and it'll kill her for sure now I'm back. So I says, make up your mind.

She still looks like she did after the funeral. Walks around all day with her mouth half open, like she's thirsty. Like an alcoholic looking for her drink. Still at the TV all night.

I must have been back about a week, down to Sobeys in the new mall, and who do I see but Jeremy. Wearing the green apron and stacking the fruits and vegetables. Mother never goes to Sobeys. She's at the Co-op every Tuesday, rain or shine. Same as always. I came home and said he's up there working, and she nodded. I said it was the baby that killed Margaret, drove her to it all those years ago. Mother shook her head with a queer look, and turned away. I was supposed to leave her alone then. But I didn't, and finally she said yes, it was the baby.

Jeremy's there every day, always on the move and ordering the rest of them around. If you ask him, he'll still price your fruits and vegetables the old-fashioned way. Put them on the scale, and watch the scale with one eye closed. Do the math in his head and write the price in a big black marker. You can add one more banana or take away a carrot and he'll do it again. Give you the new price in a flash. Do it in his head. He still lives with his grandparents and walks home at the end of the day, up behind the mall. But he doesn't walk. He runs. Every day he's out the door and off like a shot. The other night I was out on Bennett Drive, and he flew right by me with a big grin on his face and the yellow hair bouncing in his eyes. Not much weight on him, and the one foot still turned nearly sideways. But he can motor.

The highway's long since paved over. You'd never know anything happened. People are always getting killed and they just clean it up and carry on. There was a feller killed the other day out around Springdale. It was on the news. They showed the wreck. Big old F-150. Someone was on crying and saying what a fine young man he was. Makes you wonder what kind of mess he got himself into before the accident. He's probably better off. They're all better off.

I went in for a check-up last week. They made me stay all day and shot the enema into me and did the x-ray. At the end of it they said I got a black spot right down below. I said how big is it, and the doctor said it's small. As big as a dime? No, he said, not even that. I'm going back on Monday and they'll know what it is.

Jeremy will be twenty-two in the fall. Older than Margaret. She was a couple of weeks short of twenty-two when Nate Cumby's Camaro went off the highway. That's a long life for someone in his condition. The doctor said so when he was born, that the best they could expect was a few years. He's well past that now. He'll slow down, and then his body will go just like that. It'll take him in a hurry. I should go down to Sobeys and tell him. We're in the same boat now. Me and you, Jeremy. It's coming for you in a hurry, and I got the black spot and we'll see what they say on Monday. So it might be coming for me as well. Everyone got to pay for their sins.

Rescue

Carrie Ivardi

LAYLA IS CROUCHED beneath the sharp jut of rock that angles toward the sky. Adam can make her out, just barely, in the lulls when the snow settles. He's strapping the injured snowboarder to the toboggan but turns his head to look up the hill. Gusts of wind blow across the flat top of the mountain, pouring snow down over Layla's head.

Layla stands. Arms out in a surfer's pose, rocking a little to ease her snowboard forward. Adam suspects she's making a move to position herself below the toboggan to help stabilize it, but he's already maneuvering into a snow plough and is starting to make his way down.

"Adam!" Her voice is a snow gun going off in his head. He looks around and sees the slab of compressed ice and snow break off beneath her snowboard. It's gliding ahead of her over the powdery layer, a car with no brakes, heading straight for Adam and the injured rider on the toboggan.

Earlier, Adam had seen Layla at the bottom of the hill between the ticket booths and ski lifts when Kyle cut him off. Hip cocked, one arm hugging her board, her other hand massaging her cheek with a guitar pick.

Kyle was having a hard time between gasps and nose wiping to explain what the matter was. Layla's hand pressed the pick into the flesh below her cheekbone and Kyle got his point across: his brother was stranded somewhere up in Harmony Bowl. Adam led Kyle to the front of the gondola line and Layla was there, in a waft of pomegranate lotion and beeswax lip balm. She shook off both mittens, unzipped her pocket to put the pick away.

Adam didn't want to look at her. Kyle had said his brother told him he was fine. Adam had an obligation to see for himself. He stared through the scratched Plexiglas window at the view, layers of mountain peaks and winding valleys doused in white and green, revealing itself above the stubborn layer of fog still clinging to the valley. Adam spoke without looking at Layla.

"It's not going to make any difference."

"But you knew I'd be here."

Kyle had stopped sniffing and started slapping his hand against his thigh. Probably anxious about the half-hour gondola ride. Kyle eyed the symbolic cross on Adam's patroller jacket before lighting a joint. His shoulders were hunched, and his dark hair frothed out from under his helmet. "My mom's gonna kill me. Fuck."

Layla turned her back on Adam when Kyle offered her the joint. The spliff hissed and glowed, hissed and glowed, and Kyle's hand shook during the pass.

"Where'd I know you from again?" Layla asked Kyle.

"We met at Tommy Africa's, remember?"

Adam remembered. He chuckled to himself, smugly, because Layla'd had to ask Kyle his name before. She'd told Adam months ago she was done with stoner snowboarder types.

"So who's hurt?"

Kyle took the last drag, licked his fingers and pinched the end, then stuffed the roach into his empty smoke pack.

"My brother. Shit, Mom'll kill me, anything happens to him."

"I think it already did, bro," said Adam.

Kyle groaned like a child with a tummy ache and rubbed a hand up and down one side of his face.

Adam focused on the razor-sharp peaks Layla had once compared to actors appearing and reappearing from behind a curtain of weather. She moved closer to him and opened her mouth, that silent gasp of awe he knew she reserved for the view. He expected her to break out in that honky-tonk version of Fats Domino's "Blueberry Hill," the way she did when he met her. It was a First-Aid course he was teaching. She showed up ten minutes late, her guitar case clenched under her arm the way some people carry a briefcase. She croaked a verse of the song out during the unit on how to tie a sling, and then broke into a snorting laugh. Adam chose her as his casualty to demonstrate First Aid for choking, the insides of his arms snug against her abdomen.

The gondola swayed and Layla stepped closer to him, close enough that he imagined her heat, that constant vibration she emitted, bouncing like sound waves off his sleeve. He concentrated on the flotilla of mountains unfolding as they climbed higher on the cables.

"The topography of climate, eh?" she said.

Adam pulled his arm across his chest. He touched his mouth with one finger, assumed the stance of the First-Aid instructor three years her senior. Kyle was busy babbling a soundtrack of curse prayers to his mother, and Adam didn't want to have this conversation in front of him.

Her voice was soft, and he thought, maybe she's acting out this calmness, which he found more alarming than the raw, pleading way she'd attacked him the night before, saying, "Fuck it. Love is like a job. It's easier to find another when you already have one." But he didn't recall either of them, throughout this whole season of tangling themselves in each other's limbs, ever mentioning anything about love.

Maybe she believed he'd change his mind. He had a selfish

desire for her to pine for him, look out to the horizon of his departure and wait for him to come back over the mountains.

"At least look at me."

He did. Her cheeks were flushed, the wild glow in her eyes that bore into him like that night under the single bare bulb in his room before she shaded them with her hand.

He'd already started packing. The job is in South America where he will measure the topography of climate. There's an accountability about weather he appreciates. Weather has a personality, completely affected by the landscape in which it operates. It's the one controlling factor in everything, rescue, movement of people.

"Adam…my guts are in knots."

Her gaze was a flare that burnt him before he could look away, seek out the peak of Black Tusk over there to the south. He held the railing as the gondola lurched, braced his thighs against the rushing sense of arrival at the top. He stepped across the threshold as soon as the door slid open, retrieved his gear from the rack, clicked into his skis and headed for the traverse that leads to the Harmony Express chair.

Layla's rhythmic swishes were close behind him. He knew the outlines of the world would be softened for her by the pot, the fist-sized snowflakes blurring every tree, skier, contour of land. He wondered which of her lyrics were rolling through her head to match the motion of her body, toe edge, heel edge, toe edge. *Certain…magic…first…love…best…day…you-asshole-my-guts-in-knots…*

At the bottom she unhooked her back foot and shuffled through the ski-patroller line. Kyle grabbed her arm.

"You were wailing on the guitar at Tommy's that night, after the lights came up—"

"Oh, I didn't know you were—"

Kyle lowered his voice and Adam knew the weed had dulled Kyle's brotherly concern when he asked Layla, "What's up with him?"

She took off her mitten and reached for the pick in her pocket. "Nothing, let's go," she said, and they all got on the chair-lift.

Adam wondered what she remembered about Tommy's. After the lights came up, how she lifted her guitar out from under a table. The song about how she moved west all mixed up with lyrics about landmines. Her guitar, and a resolution to use it to get wherever she needed to go. No matter what. All of this said in a drunken stupor.

She'd been wearing her Hunter S. Thompson shades that night, and she pulled it off. She leaned over her guitar to chug the last of her beer, but she had all the drunks and druggies as well as Adam and the bartender and the bouncers completely mesmerized. On their way back to his place, her guitar case banging against her legs, he'd had to hold her up by her elbow to keep her from splatting into a snowbank.

The chair swayed slightly and Layla strummed a steady beat in the crease where her thigh almost touched his. "The drifts of snow, they're like ghosts dancing," she said. Kyle grunted agreement, mumbling to his mom or the air or both.

The first time Adam saw her perform, he'd been on cue to get her a glass of water from the bar. At the end of her set she laid her guitar to rest in its case next to the overturned beer bottles. Her elation was palpable as she glided toward him, her hair a slick, wet frame around her face. He'd held the glass out to her and she shook her head no, her fingers still busy making the shape of the chords.

The guitar had belonged to a man on a street in Toronto. The concrete buildings, the cars with their first gritty sprays of salt from the road, were monochromatic that time of year, late fall. Layla's preparation to leave completely anonymous, she said, to stake her own claim to the mythological migration of twenty-somethings heading west. A man in a puddle congealing into ice.

The lid of the guitar case was open, the finish on the guitar gleaming more brightly as the daylight faded and the streetlights made an orange haze of the fog. When she took it, she said she was calm. No sirens blaring her guilty intent. No panic rising in her guts, tripping her up. The unmoving lump of the man on the ground. The cold when she reached under the blanket, her hand on the man's chest, no rise and fall. No breath. Some of the things she said made Adam shiver.

No breath and she said she knew it wasn't just the fading light colouring his bare toes grey. Someone else had already taken his shoes. *Corpse toes like gnarled branches knotted without a name tag, faded in freezer mist.* "An Intensity of Timing," a title for the song she wrote for her guitar, sung with a fierceness that makes him question whether the shivers are cold or warm. She's superstitious about it, has only ever sung that one for him. Over and over, so that he'll never forget the lyrics. He never asked to be keeper of her song.

She chose Whistler, she'd said, for the magical combination of venues to play and snowboarding, the achievable sensation of floating. Even when she was smashed, she never told him anything more about where she came from. Like her whole entire history began with a dead guy and a guitar.

They dismounted from the chairlift. Adam fetched the rescue toboggan from a culvert, and Layla held the rope attached to the back while he gripped the handlebar to steer it from the front, his poles tucked under one arm. They paused when Kyle indicated the route he'd taken with his brother.

"I had this bad feeling today, y'know? And my mom—"

"You can stop saying that now," said Adam.

"It'll be okay," from Layla.

They had to ski down a winding trail to get to Harmony

Bowl. Layla held tight to the toboggan's rope until Adam had to either ask her to let go or engage in a tug of war with her.

"Jesus, Adam, it's not that I wanted to sit around with you until we started talking about our grey hair. But this? There's no plan for this, either."

"I told you, it's a job."

"Does it have to be so far away?" And let go.

Adam knows mathematical equations, scientific method. Applicable, functioning transitions from hypothesis to conclusion. Who is he to ponder backbeats and chord transitions, or how a song's supposed to resonate in your soul? It wasn't an impulsive decision to accept the job, his finger hovering only a moment before hitting send on the email. Impulsive is a word Layla would say about him then throw her head back and laugh. He who has been known to leave the grocery store, return with a more thorough list.

Behind him Layla was singing some new song about Adam's odour still on her skin.

"Take a picture of me," she'd said one afternoon in her room. He looked for the camera on her dresser. There was a pile of albums spread west to east: Daniel Lapp to Amelia Curran. The camera perched on a shot glass full of guitar picks.

He'd turned back to the bed and she was naked on her side, one knee over her guitar. Rubbing a finger up and over the neck, along the strings. An eerie similarity in the curve of woman and guitar that made him want to flatten her with his body, ride her frenzied motions beneath him, or throw on his boots and feel the exertion of getting to the top of the mountain by foot. He did neither. Waited for her to crawl toward him, put her mouth on him, take him inside her and dig herself in until darkness claimed the pattern of scrunched-up blankets and two bodies limp in shared, musky dampness.

Out here above the tree line there is no smell. It's not like those commercials for air fresheners, breezy scents to fill your home with the great reminiscence of the outdoors. What you smell is the saliva on your neck warmer, coffee breath and wood smoke. Old boogers on your coat where it zips and Velcros over your chin when your hood is up. You poke your nose out from under your goggles, your snot freezes.

Their last night together she'd been all over him with elbows and knees, baring teeth and tongue, moaning and crying. His mouth on hers, her fingers tough as the strings of her guitar, fists twisted in his hair, pulling him up and over her body after he'd been down on her, lover's spit trailing clammy patterns over her pubic bone, her navel, his thumb smoothing damp flesh below her ribcage. All of this in the middle of his escalating explanations and her mounting hysteria.

They reached the lip of Harmony Bowl, an endless field of powder before them. They could see Kyle's brother sitting up, relief in the arm he lifted to wave at them. Adam skied toward him to start assessing the injured knee.

Her voice is in his mind. It's not possible to discern it the usual way in this wind. His body a conduit, the sensation of thousands of needles sticking him in every pore, every nerve ending, every fleck of bone. He wonders if this is what any human body feels like just before a leg breaks or a spine cracks. Before he shows up for the rescue.

He watches the movement of the slab of snow, white on white, with a sort of detachment. He's prepared to move but pauses to look up the hill at her. Her body relaxes, then tenses. Sweat beading on her skin, wet beneath his palms. On stage, her eyes were closed, her head swayed side to side. Her right arm flew up and down, up and down, fingers of her left hand gripping, flipping, G, D, E harmonics.

She leans into the hill and Adam searches for her eyes behind her goggles. She lifts her arm to raise them off her face, her chords playing louder, faster. She leans too far. That night at Tommy's she was closed off from everything around her, he was about to reach out to feel her radiating energy when something crashed behind the bar. His body jerks as hers flips forward and she skids through the snow. A taste rises in his mouth as he skies off to one side of the ice slab, dragging the toboggan. The ice rushes past him. Above the bar a hundred bottles of booze smashed down and sent a brilliant explosion of glass across the floor. The bartender had been on the other side, mopping a spill the stragglers kept slipping in. Adam sees Kyle get away from the slab of ice on the opposite side. No pause in Layla's playing, she'd kept going as though her song had absorbed the sound, left her oblivious to anything else going on around her.

Kyle approaches Adam and the toboggan, kneels down next to his brother. Kyle, jabbing a gloved finger up inside his goggles, sniffing, gulping air, one hand on his brother's chest.

She's belly flopped and flailing to dig herself out of the deep snow, instinctively pulling her knees into her chest. Her tongue sweeping the helix of his ear, she'd said, "I may never make it in the world of music. But you'll never find a better lay." The two most coherent sentences she ever uttered that time of night. Her face burrows in the powder before she gets her hands under her shoulders to push herself up, every muscle in him braced in her struggle. She manages a squat. Her board wants to ride the powder but her body isn't ready. The sensation in his mouth is like the first metal taste of regret.

He calls out a name. The decision already made. He told her once that if you're ever lost, the best thing to do is stay put. A lesson from kindergarten, she added. Stay in one place and you'll eventually be found. He watches her catch two syllables on her tongue, slide several meters before somersaulting. She lands on all fours facing downhill. He can feel her shudders.

He breathes evenly again as she straightens her goggles on her face. The drifts of snow have stopped their dancing, and her arm in the air stirs the few remaining snowflakes. Above, the stratus coverage starts to break apart into fluffy cumulus clouds.

He said, "Sometimes we're better off..." The words he'd planned about making a clean break no longer make any sense. The way a storm sweeping across a landscape will alter the mood of its topography temporarily, but knocks down a permanent feature, a giant spruce or a building, changing something essential about it forever.

Over the trails, across the valley, past the chairlifts and the moving dots of skiers, there's a line separating snow from trees on the adjacent mountains. Black Tusk juts into the sky, a marker to the right of the setting sun. The serrated peaks behind it seem to shift in the passing clouds. He watches her body recover, start to ride down the hill. He steers the toboggan, her music still in his head.

A Holy Show

Melanie Oates

I FOUND HIM at Holy Show. The friggin Irish bar where a bottle of beer costs eight dollars. Out dancing he was, with this missus I recognized from up the shore. Short blue dress with ruffles around the neck and brown boots to her knees. He had that rotten black beanie hanging off his head and a white t-shirt with something spilled all down the front. I turned into the bar and ordered a pint.

A tap on my shoulder and a squeal. This Ashley that went from kindergarten to grade twelve with me. Ashley plus fifty pounds and still wearing the same clothes. She started in on the catch up game. I was real friendly and interested. At the end of the song, while everyone clapped politely, there was a roar from the front of the stage. Halt with his two arms up in the air like ladders, barking at the band.

Look at the state of that fella, Ashley said. He's in here the whole night. Different girl out to every song. He's about one dance away from being thrown out, I'd say. What about you, Devi, do you have either man these days? Halt spots me then. Bulldozed through the crowd. Locked his arms around my waist and lifted my face to reach his and kissed me.

Oh, Ashley said.

What're ya doing here, dolly? he asked.

Just dropped in to see my old friend from home, Ashley, I said.

He let me down and held his hand out to her. She eyed it.

Nice to meet ya, Ash.

She gave him her hand and took it back quick.

Who are you?

Tommy Halt.

Oh yeah, I heard tell of you before.

His usual scruff had turned into a beard since I'd seen him last. Paths of blood vessels around his eyes. He was grabbing at me. His face into my neck, licking me. Ashley shook her head and left.

You tracked me down, he said.

I thought you might be after doin away with yourself.

I'm too fond of myself for that.

Can we leave?

You can leave. I'm havin a time.

Havin a time at Holy Show? Havin a time, are ya?

You gonna have a dance with me?

That's what I'm not.

Stubborn as a stop sign.

When the hubby's-night-out crew cleared away from the bar, I managed to snag a stool. The band started playing "Will Ye Go Lassie Go" and Halt was leaning on a table full of scrots. The friends were nudging this one girl and she got up, blushing, and went to waltz with him. As if he knows how to waltz now. But he did. The old-fashioned waltz. Singing out the words and twirling her around for fuck's sakes. He didn't so much as glance at me.

He shoots out for a smoke then, in his bare arms, when the song is over. Three of them from the scrot table, with one dress between them, scurry out behind him. I think about picking up some food and going home out of it. I half-watched them through the window. Him and the three of them standing in a little group. Four fellas, two in snowmobiling jackets, two in wool jackets, standing behind them pointing and nodding their heads at Halt. Knows there's not going to be a racket tonight.

This lumpy, soggy fella sidles up beside me offering drinks and I tell him I'm underage. Halt brings an armload of drinks from the bar to the scrot table. Shots and red things with ice and straws. Watched him put the straws in the glasses myself. They has a little cheers then. He says something grotesque, no doubt, and they kills their selves laughing. And even in his dirtbag state, he's only the best thing I've ever seen.

I took the path that went by the scrot table on my way to the bathroom. Glaring at one of the girls while she's leaning into him.

I met him on my way out.

You're still here?

The ends of his words were mushed.

I'm havin a drink with some girls from home, I told ya.

Come and sit with us.

With us? Imagine. It was a task not to tear a piece out of her but I wasn't giving him the satisfaction.

Do your thing.

I heard him give the bathroom door a boot. That was just him being playful.

I plopped down next to Ashley and her friends from university. She didn't look too pleased about it. But that was it now, wasn't it.

Is Tommy Halt your boyfriend or something?

Not really. Kind of. We're screwin around, I s'pose.

Isn't he s'posed to be a bit of an idiot?

He is, yeah.

What's he at with all them girls? That skinny blonde one on the end by him? I knows her. She's friends with my friend Sandra. She was at Sandra's bachelorette party there the summer. She's a hardcore skank. Got ossified on the Party Bus and puked all over the seat. Still went to the bar. I heard she made out with the groom.

You have either fella on the go?

She shifted into me, pleased to talk about it. Remember Adam, she said. He was a few years ahead of us in school. They're engaged now. Building a house. She showed me her white-gold band with one chocolate chip sized diamond in the middle.

In Halt's absence, the b'ys from outside moved in on the scrot table. The scrots were a hit! He came out screaming along the words to whatever the band was playing. They eyed him and just wanted to slit his throat or whatever the polo shirt version of that is. Halt put his arm around one of them, a short fella. Said something to him and flipped his collar down. They scattered back to the bar.

Out for a smoke and the four boys came out behind me.

How ya tonight, b'ys?

I moved into their circle. Chatted them up for a bit. This one, Chris or Kevin, I can't remember, said he loved my hair and ran his hand down through it. I nestled into the bar with them after that. Two on each side. Halt glanced at me then. Friggin easy. He squat in on the end of Chris/Kevin. Didn't speak to me and ordered another round of drinks.

Who's that fella? Chris asked when he left.

Some poet. S'posed to be a hard ticket, I say.

Hear that boys, he said, a poet.

It was a little joke.

On our way to the dance floor for a scuff, I nails the blonde with my shoulder coming back from the bathroom. Her red drink runs down the front of her pink dress.

What the fuck? Watch where you're going.

You knocked into me, ya louse. Think now, which kind of stain is harder to get out, blood or cranberry juice?

She waited, and decided, good thing, to keep moving along. Chris gave me a grin. She was telling Halt what happened. Pointing at me. He wiped her tits down with a napkin.

Ashley and her gaggle were dancing by me and the boys. She bent into me and said, You're really trying to start an uproar. You're still the same Devi.

I resented that. I was just worried about Halt and now here I was. Doing what? What was I at, exactly?

I grabbed my jacket and scarf. Enough of that racket. Halt was out smoking again. Just him and her this time. That's the one, there, that ruined my dress, she said. He grinned at me.

Where ya goin?

What do you care? The fuck out of here.

The blonde crossed her arms, confused.

You're not bringin one of them fraternity brothers with ya?

No. Me and you don't operate under the same style.

What style is that?

Skank.

Tommy. This is the bitch that ran into me.

His name is Halt. Halt.

And what are you? Like his little stalker fangirl or something? Rammed my hands into her chest. She went staggering back. Came at me. I grabbed her by the hair of her head. Her nails went into my cheek. Halt laughed.

Get away from me, I told her. I'm not goin havin a bitch fight. You. I haven't been able to get ahold of you for days. I thought you were fuckin overdosed or dead. All you're at is dancin at Holy Show. How many days have ya been on it? How many days have ya been loaded now?

How many days you been barfing now?

Only every once in a while when I thinks of your face.

But here ya are. Out hunting me.

Don't worry. Won't happen again. The crows will have your eyeballs picked out before I goes lookin for ya again, you dirty drunk. Hey missus, I hope you're alright with takin a scattered beatin. And don't bother with a condom. I'm sure he's clean.

Well I'd only have whatever you're after givin me, ragdoll. And missy. No I'm not a fangirl. I was his girlfriend.

He went to bolt. Missus chased after him.

Tommy, where are you going? I'm coming.

Will you shag off girl and go fuck one of them collared queers. I've been on the booze for four days. My dick's no good to ya.

She came sulking back, looking at me. I spit, just missing her foot.

Dirtbag, she said under her breath.

I stopped into the Jester. Just got in before they locked the door. Sat by myself. No one really around. I was sad for him. It wasn't about me. He wasn't doing it to me. He was doing it to himself. Or it was happening to him.

Walking home, after four in the morning, there he was passed out on the step of the Vessel with neither jacket on, but drink still in his hand. I shook him. Nothing. I yelled at him. Nothing. I sat on him, facing him. Wrapped my arms and legs around him. Blew my hot breath on his neck. Nothing. I took his face in my hands and shook his head. He took me in and flinched back.

Jesus. What's on the go?

You're passed out on the street. That's what. You're half froze to death.

He brought the drink to his mouth. Coughed and it dribbled down his chin. I wrapped my scarf around him. He didn't fight me.

Come on. Get up now, ya big brute.

I had him up. His weight clumsy on me. We fell.

Jesus. Stand up. Stand up would ya?

I am. I'm standin. I'm standin.

I jumped at a cab going by. Buddy wasn't too keen on letting Halt in. Would only take him as long as he was able to get in and out by himself.

I'm not going lugging him, he said.

Neither am I, I told him.

Get in girl.

Not gettin in.

Please, Devi. You're a…you're a…

I'm a what?

You're a…an alien.

Honest to god.

No. You're a…you're just an astronaut that's never been to space.

What are you gettin on with? Go home and go to bed.

Go on then, cabbie. And if you're not with me, Devi, would you at least schedule me a lobotomy cause that's the only way I'll suffer it without you, I swear.

I flagged a cab and called the pizza guy on the way home. Yes please, supersize. Yes to the garlic fingers. All of the dipping sauces. You take credit cards, right? Yeah, they do.

I beat him there, man with pizza, and swung the cupboard doors open like the legs of a working girl, threw my hand in there and grabbed. Whatever came out I pushed into my mouth while I groped at the clothes I was wearing until they surrendered themselves to the floor. Back into the boxers and tank top, tying my hair up and back while hitting the power button on the television. Filled up the jug with water and stationed it within reach of my spot on the couch. Just in time—knock knock.

The delivery guy was about my age, maybe a bit older, tall, husky, bearded. Looked like the real skeet, ball cap on and jacket flung open. He glared at me with a half-smile. A real prick too. $35.80.

I held out my credit card.

I don't take them.

When I called they told me you did.

No. If you want to use your credit card you have to do it over the phone. I don't take em at the door.

To get rid of him, that's all I wanted. Just leave me and my pizza.

Should I call them back then?

He grunted a yes.

He was gawking at my skin, all of it, wanting me to know that he wasn't afraid to look.

I went to the phone, thinking that he would stay standing in the doorframe while I called, but he followed me in. The door banged shut behind him. I don't know why I didn't say anything. Just allowed him in.

I dialed the pizza place, trying to act all casual and in control while thinking in my head, my god, I'm about to be raped. I can't believe I'm about to be raped. I hope it's just rape at least, and not murder. When he comes at you, go for the groin and the eyeballs with all you got.

Nobody was answering on the other end. His eyes, looking up from under his eyebrows, ate my skin. He came closer. Then I remembered.

I have cash in there. You wait right here. One second.

Hands shivering, I slid two twenties out of a drawer and said, Johnny? Johnny, wake up. The pizza is here, loud enough to be heard in the other room. I pushed my hands into the mattress to make it sound like somebody was moving around.

Who are you talking to?

I give him the forty dollars.

My boyfriend. He passed out while we were waiting for the pizza.

He held my eye, looking for a sign of a lie while I tried to keep my lungs still. I tipped him.

Keep the change. Sorry for the misunderstanding.

I tipped him. And I apologized.

I held the door open, he made sure his shoulder pushed into mine as he passed through. He groaned and gave me one last eye over.

With the deadbolt jammed into the hole, I knelt in front of the couch, arms and face pressed into the cushion and screamed. You'd think that I would have taken it as some kind of sign from somewhere. Should have thrown that pizza over the deck and never again would I even think about gorging like a gull. I choked it down on top of the jaggy tears until it disappeared and then reappeared, mashed up and wet, as I looked down at it. Pulled the handle and the sludge was swallowed down.

A toilet can take just about anything.

KC
Accidental

Morgan Murray

KC WAS HIT by a bus—the Number Seven, one of the city's busiest, which ran from Fortune City Mall to Vagrant Village, the trailer park where he grew up and his mother still lived—on a Wednesday while trying to cross Milton Street just after lunch. He was carrying a six-foot fake Christmas tree under one arm and trying to send a text message to his mother with the other. He had glanced up from his phone and to his right, but not his left, as he stepped off the curb and in front of the three-quarters full Number Seven. The wallop stopped his heart instantly, and that was it for KC.

There wasn't much left of KC. His body and belongings littered Milton Street as if a pack of dogs had torn someone's garbage bags apart—bits strewn down the block, being blown by passing traffic back up onto the sidewalk. Of what remained, one of the most substantial, and certainly the thing that left the most lasting impression, was KC's man-sized oblong smear on the asphalt. And even that wouldn't last long.

The officer in charge of the aftermath, Staff Sergeant Dover, had been on the force for nineteen years, every last one of them in the Traffic Division, and was a family man—proud father of Pat, eleven, Quinn, twelve, and Sandy, thirteen. So he decided that a man-sized oblong smear was an inappropriate thing to have on Milton Street in front of the Merry Munchkin Daycare Centre. There wasn't much he could do about the forty-three merry munchkins who'd watched KC step out in front of the Number Seven moments after they'd been sent outside following lunch—Wednesday being chicken nugget day. Nor could he do much for the twenty-four third-graders from Ms. Polliston's Blaise Pascal Elementary School class who were riding the Number Seven as part of a class project on public transportation. But damned if Staff Sergeant Dover was going to subject anymore children to the sight of something as horrendous as a man-sized oblong smear on Milton Street.

While EMTs Blumb and Seibert and Constables Dean and Turvill busied themselves collecting the bits of KC and KC's things off of Milton Street, Staff Sergeant Dover called the fire department to get them to come blast the KC smear off the street.

Blasting a man-sized oblong KC smear off of Milton Street, however, was a ways down the fire department's priority list.

District Chief Simpson told Staff Sergeant Dover as much when he first got the call. Constable Dean, loading an armload of KC into the ambulance, overheard Staff Sergeant Dover screaming into his cellphone something about, "I don't give two fucks if you do take it to the D. Comm."—D. Comm. stood for District Commander, District Chief Simpson's superior—"there's a bunch of kids here bawling their eyes out over what they just saw. I need you lazy pricks to get down here and blast 'im off the goddamned street."

Staff Sergeant Dover was, of course, wrong. He was wrong to swear at District Chief Simpson, wrong to insinuate all firemen were "lazy pricks," or pricks at all, and wrong to even call the fire department in the first place. Blasting man-sized KC smears off of city streets was the jurisdiction of the police's Crime Scene Sanitation Division. Staff Sergeant Dover knew all of this, he had been on the force for nineteen years after all, every last one of them in the Traffic Division, he had seen his share of horrors, but this was just too much. The sight of those forty-three terrified munchkins who had just seen KC eat it—cheeks streaked with tears and sticky, blood-red sweet and sour sauce—was just too much for him.

But, no amount of begging, pleading, or good goddamns from Staff Sergeant Dover could convince District Chief Simpson—a real by-the-book man—to bend protocol. So the Traffic Division kept Milton Street closed until rush hour and KC's memorial man-sized oblong smear remained until mid-morning the next day when the Crime Scene Sanitation Division finally got around to it. By then it was more of a smudge.

By the time three Crime Scene Sanitation Technicians in yellow rubber HAZMAT suits armed with two pressure washers and one long-handled scrub brush got around to blasting KC's smudge off Milton Street, that was really all that was left of him. He was cremated, by accident, in Thursday's wee hours, when Goolie's Funeral Home, where he was being put back together ahead of his Friday funeral—his mother, staunchly Catholic, insisted on a proper burial for her son—burned to the ground. By the time District Chief Simpson's trucks from Fire Houses Eleven and Nineteen had gotten the fire out, KC's ashes, and those of the seven other corpses, including one belonging to the previously undeceased undertaker Melvin Goolie, had mingled with the ash and rubble from the sixty-year-old funeral home with the faulty viewing-room wiring, and it was impossible to tell whose were whose.

KC's mother, without a KC to bury, buried what KC had with him when he went. At least what hadn't been lost in the Goolie's Fire. Which was quite a lot thanks to EMTs Blumb and Seibert, Constables Dean and Turvill, and Staff Sergeant Dover, in all of the excitement Wednesday afternoon, mistakenly sending most of KC's things to the Evidence Handling Division instead of Goolie's

Funeral Home with KC. What was to be KC until the end of time amounted to a badly stained pair of blue jeans, size thirty-one-thirty-two; a pair of patent leather loafers with the right sole worn through, size nine; a nylon wallet with Velcro® closure containing a bank card, a driver's license, a health insurance card, a social insurance card, a gas station rewards points card, an expired condom, a receipt for $27.45 worth of groceries, an expired ten percent off coupon for laser printer toner from Print Heaven on Willbury Street, and five dollars cash; a broke-in-two cellphone with a faulty six key; a forest green windbreaker/rain jacket with detachable hood, which conveniently folds into the left pocket, unfolded; spare change: a quarter, a dime, and two pennies; a knapsack containing a tattered secondhand copy of *The Road* by Cormac McCarthy, a blank notebook with the first page torn out, a pair of bicycle shorts, a sweat-stained grey t-shirt with "I Survived Thunder Camp 1998" printed in faded blue letters across the chest, a pair of dirty running shoes with a flappy right sole, size nine-and-a-half, a crumpled chocolate-bar wrapper, and half a pack of long lasting winter mint gum; a key ring with three keys—two for building door locks, and one for a car ignition—a remote locking device for some sort of small import car, and a key tag for entry into Rock Hard Gym; and a six-foot fake Christmas Tree. It amounted to enough to fill a casket nearly full, though KC's mother saved about $200 thanks to the casket that fit KC's things being a bit smaller than one that would have fit KC.

KC's mother learned of KC's end the usual way.

After overseeing the evacuation of the Merry Munchkin Daycare Centre and the closure of Milton Street, and after giving interviews to media at the scene, Staff Sergeant Dover left Constable Dean in charge of supervising the towing of the Number Seven to the depot and drove the remainder the Number Seven's usual route to Vagrant Village Trailer Park— named, half-jokingly, for the Depression-era tent city that used to be on the site, made famous by the 1961 novel based on its 1934 cholera outbreak *Run City Run* by Rudy Ellington.

The clomping of Staff Sergeant Dover's giant boots on the rotting front step of trailer thirty-seven followed by the teeth-grinding creek of the storm door woke KC's mother—the night dishwasher at Uncle Tucky's All-Night Diner. She was out of bed, into her housecoat, and grumbling "Who in the—?" down the hall before the first knock came. "Who is it?"

"Ma'am, it's Staff Sergeant Dover of the City Police." KC's mother could see, through the yellow lace curtain, Staff Sergeant Dover was hat in hand. "Ma'am, may I—" she didn't hear another word, everything went grey and began to spin and vibrate, her ears began to ring, her stomach, and its contents, leapt into her throat, her legs went soft.

Staff Sergeant Dover let himself in though the unlocked door after there was no response to several more calls. As soon as he opened the door the smell of cigarettes, mothballs, bacon fat, and cheap whiskey hit him. He found KC's mother in what he took to be the living room. The room was heavy with a damp greyness, the yellowed floral wallpaper was peeling at the seams and in the corners. Surrounded by piles of old newspapers, flyers, catalogues, and empty cigarette cartons, KC's mother sat in a stained grey-brown-orange recliner that didn't recline anymore, with a lit cigarette in her left hand. Her mouth hung open. Her eyes were glassy, and red. Tears streamed down her cheeks.

Staff Sergeant Dover stood frozen, staring at her for the longest time. She didn't move. He explained: "Your son, KC, was hit by a city bus today while crossing Milton Street, he died instantly, he did not suffer ma'am." She did not move. "My condolences, ma'am." She didn't move. "I'm a father myself—three: eleven, twelve, and thirteen. It's the damnedest thing, ma'am." She didn't move. "We've collected KC and his belongings, we'll need to have someone come down and identify his body." She didn't move. "It's the damnedest thing ma'am." She didn't move. "I am so sorry for your loss, ma'am." She didn't move. Staff Sargent Dover shook his head slowly and shuck-shucked at the tragedy. She didn't move. "A real tragedy, ma'am." She didn't move. He had run out of things to say so he just stood shucking and shaking. She didn't move. Shucking and shaking. She didn't move. Her cigarette burned itself out and a long rainbow of ash fell off the butt and onto the arm of the chair. She didn't move. Shucking and shaking. She didn't move. When, mid-shuck, KC's mother shuddered, sucked snot back into her nose with all the force, violence, and noise of a wood chipper, and sobbed "Ca-argh-rrrrl!" Staff Sergeant Dover nearly had a heart attack.

The snort and sob brought KC's mother back. Now she sobbed and convulsed and wailed. Staff Sergeant Dover was much more comfortable with this. Nineteen years on the force, every last one of them in the Traffic Division, he'd seen his share of grief-stricken mothers. This was usually the point where he'd pat the mother on the shoulder and move on with things. But KC's mother was sequestered in her trash fortress. He sidled past a pile of old *TV Guides*, inching his way closer to the chair, crunching cigarette cartons and cellophane under his giant boots. "It's a damned tragedy, ma'am," he shucked, shook, and sidled, while she sobbed and snorted. He was caught in awkward limbo again, trying desperately to get over to console her, so he could get on with things. "Damned tragedy." He kicked over a stack of Sears catalogues. Several years' worth helicoptered off the pile. Spring 1997 ricocheted off a yellow laundry basket full of yellowed *Criers* and crashed into the TV table KC's mother had her ashtray on. The legs of the table buckled, tossing the ashtray and several weeks' worth of KC's mother's chain-smoked butts flipping in a graceful arc over the arm of the chair and into her lap. The cloud of ash that went with it gently settled, covering her and the stained grey-brown-orange recliner that didn't recline anymore in a fine grey-black dust.

KC's funeral was held at Our Lady of Perpetual Suffering Roman Catholic Church on Fort Apt Avenue, first thing Friday morning. The priest, Father Lucius Garrire, wanted to get through it quickly, as he had Melvin Goolie's funeral and a baptism to get through that morning before the monthly Catholic Women's League Luncheon at the Knights of Columbus Hall on Holloway Street at one o'clock—which, for him, was the most emotionally draining of all his regular monthly social events, though the food was usually pretty good.

Our Lady of Perpetual Suffering, the fourth oldest in the diocese, was originally built during the Depression as an equipment shed for the Department of Transport's growing make-work fleet. During the war it was annexed by the Department of Defence and turned into a munitions factory, building the recoil dampening springs and trigger mechanisms for the FG-44 rifle, a semi-automatic rifle that never saw any action because of jamming problems. After the building sat vacant for more than a decade after the war the Department of Defence sold the rifle spring and trigger factory to the St. Ignatius Arch-Diocese for a token dollar, though no money ever did change hands.

The Diocese Association then set to raising the money to renovate the old factory into a church. They first had a frame built around the main smoke stacks to give the appearance of a steeple, then they had the building stuccoed, inside and out, to give the beam and girder sheet metal building more of a churchish look.

Before too many years passed they had the giant factory parti-
tioned into all sorts of chapels and confessionals, parish offices, a
rectory, a vestibule, and a large hall for A.A. meetings, prayer groups,
Wednesday night bingo, and Tuesday and Thursday afternoon soup
kitchen services, and an expansive nave with thirty-foot ceilings.
Several Knights of Columbus then travelled to the Southern States
to purchase, at a Southern Baptist church liquidation auction, the
impossibly long, and impossibly uncomfortable wooden pews to fill
the nave. The Church was officially opened, named for the Blessed
Virgin Mary's sorrowful watch over the suffering of the war dead,
once the secondhand pews arrived in seven flatbed truckloads.
From that point, every dollar from the collection plate poured
into adorning the nave with twenty-two statues of different sizes,
eighteen of them of Mary, and erecting a proper sanctuary filled
with alters and lecterns and choir stands adorned with the
customary amount of ornate woodwork, all overseen by a twelve-
foot statue of the crucified Christ.

But the most impressive part of Our Lady of Perpetual Suffering, to the hundreds of tourists who flocked to see them each
year at least, were the elaborate stained-glass scenes of martyrdom
that replaced, gradually as money would allow, the sixty-four
louvered factory windows. Sixty-four windows beautifully
decorated with executions of every imaginable sort of sixty-four
saints no one had ever heard of: St. Abundius, St. Adrio, St. Alban,
St. Alexander, St. Aphrodisius, St. Apollonius, St. Apollinaris Franco,

St. Atticus, St. Augulus, St. Basileus, St. Belina, St. Boniface, St. Candida, St. Daniel, St. Devota, St. Diomedes, St. Dionysius, St. Edmund the Martyr, St. Edward the Martyr, St. Epimachus, St. Eupsychius, St. Eutychius, St. Eutychius of Alexandria, St. Exuperius, St. Faustus, St. Flavius, St. Francis of St. Bonaventure, St. Francis of St. Mary, St. Francis of St. Michael, St. Gabinus, St. Gaius Francis, St. Gonzaga Gonza, St. Gorgias, St. Gundenis, St. Heliconis, St. Hermione, St. Hippolytus, St. Honorius, St. Humphrey Lawrence, St. Julius, St. Just, St. Juventius, St. Leocadia, St. Leocrita, St. Lucretia, St. Luxorius, St. Maurus, St. Maxellendis, St. Maximus, St. Moses, St. Octavian, St. Palmatius, St. Panacea, St. Pancratius, St. Peter Chanel, St. Plutarch, St. Polycarp of Alexandria, St. Polyeuctus, St. Pompeius of Pavia, St. Pontius of Cimella, St. Potitus, St. Theodemir, St. Warinus, and St. Zoilus.

The window scenes were based on artwork submitted as part of a contest for students at Sacred Heart of Solitude High School. The students were asked to illustrate the martyrdom of any martyred saint they wished—most choosing obscure saints with the least amount of biographical details to allow for the most imaginative interpretations of their martyrdoms. In all there were eighteen beheadings, in all manners from axe to guillotine; sixteen burnings, mostly staked; thirteen crucifixions, both traditional Jesus-style (right-side-up), eight, and the less-orthodox Peter-style (upside-down), five; twelve of the more medieval variety executions, including five drawn and quarters, four broken on the wheel, two flayings, and one boiling in oil; four stonings; and one—St. Gundenis—depicted, completely inaccurately, as the final scene from the movie Scarface, but instead of a machine gun, St. Gundenis is beckoning to his executioners to say hello to his little cross. Between Hughie Loomis' sophomoric sense of humour, his questionable artistic talents, and the contest judging panel—a bishop, two priests, two nuns, three Knights of Columbus, and three ladies from the Catholic Women's League— not being as up-to-date on famous gangster movie death scenes as they could have been, the St. Gundenis window had been paid for and installed before anyone noticed the similarity. The winners, even Hughie Loomis, all received a medal, a certificate, their name on a plaque beneath their window, a trip, during school hours, to the factory to see how the windows were made, and twenty-five dollars. Hughie Loomis also received the additional prize of a month in afterschool detention.

Yet, for all the stained-glass and stucco splendour that Our Lady of Perpetual Suffering had become, no number of contractors brought in by the Diocese Association could figure out proper ventilation for the church, so on the morning of KC's funeral, even with the main doors held open by hymnals and a half-dozen strategically placed oscillating fans going full blast, sitting in the church was like sitting in a sealed Tupperware container left on the dash of a car in full sun.

Sealed in KC's funeral were about eighty-seven people scattered through the forty rows of impossibly uncomfortable pews in the massive nave making it seem like the church was empty. Of those in attendance, seventy percent were friends of KC, twenty-nine percent friends of KC's mother, plus the two elderly ladies, Estelle and Sophia, both in their eighties, who attend every service at Our Lady of Perpetual Suffering, regardless the occasion. Estelle and Sophia sat, without exception, including KC's funeral, in the foremost right-hand pew muttering the rosary to themselves, the Blessed Virgin, and most of the congregation, for the duration, regardless the hymn, homily, or responsorial psalm being spoken or sung by the rest of the congregation or priest. It annoyed the hell out of Father Lucious when Estelle's and Sophia's muttered Hail Marys would trip him up mid-*Sanctus* and he'd include one too many Holy Holys, or one Hosanna not enough, making an ass of himself in front of the entire congregation. When this happened he'd glare red-faced for a split second at the two, think to himself, "For the love of God, shut the fuck up, you old crows," and then go back to try and find his place. Funerals were particularly bad. Between his under-familiarity with the text, and the dead silence of small, somber, funeral crowds, Father Lucious' missteps would ricochet around the old gun factory, emphasizing his incompetence. And KC's funeral, with the heat and impending luncheon weighing on Father Lucious, was particularly bad, even for funerals.

"In the name of the…uh…Father, Son, and…uh…Holy Spirit," Father Lucious stammered through his first line, shooting s.t.f.u. death stares at Estelle and Sophia who were loudly rounding their first Sorrowful Mystery, at least ten Hail Marys deep by this point. The entire congregation, following Father Lucious' lead, stammered along, not missing an um or an uh. "Saint… Saint…uh…Pa-Paul, in his epi—Saint Paul, in his second epistle to the Thessa—pardon me, Paul's first letter to the Thistle…uh… Thistle…uh…"

"Thessalonians," eleven-year-old altar server, Rory, holding a long tapered candle before the altar, whispered at Father Lucious. "Thessalonians!"

The most difficult though, of all elocutionary difficulties Father Lucious suffered through that morning, though, was KC's name itself. The missal, in a blatant attempt to trip up Father Lucious, noted the spots in the text where he was to say KC's name with a single, bolded, uppercase N. And that was it. N. *We gather here, dear friends, on this solemn occasion, to celebrate the passing of our brother/sister N into the arms of the Lord* was supposed to be read as *We gather here, dear friends, on this solemn occasion to celebrate the passing of our brother KC into the arms of the Lord.* But, by the time Father Lucious got through with it, it was more like: "We gather here, dear…uh…friends, on this solemn occasion, to celebrate the…uh…passing of our brother-sister N…KC… uh…into the arms of the…uh…Ca–KC…uh…Lord."

The funeral mass, meant to celebrate the life of KC, and give comfort to, at the very least, KC's staunchly Catholic and very bereaved mother, became in the hands of Father Lucious a funeral...uh...mass celebrating the death of brother-sister N. KC. Or, on multiple occasions brother-sister N. Clarke, N. Crake, N. Cart, more than once N. Christ, and a couple of times, in anticipation for his next funeral that morning, brother-sister N. Melvin.

After a not entirely graceless homily about the tragedy of sudden life...uh...death, and the eternal promise of the insurrection... uh...resurrection of KC...er...Christ, and an equally bungled Liturgy of the Eucharist, Father Lucious breathed a heavy sigh of relief when the final hymn, "Were You There When They Nailed Him to the Tree," kicked up and the six pallbearers—KC's uncle Randy, KC's cousins Charlie, Larry, Louis, and Gino, and KC's best-friend Morton—whisked KC's casket, full of everything KC except KC, down the aisle and out into a waiting U-Haul Van, a stand-in, provided by the insurance company, for the hearses lost in the Goolie's Fire the day before.

KC's KC-less casket was driven, through the last remnants of morning rush hour, seventeen blocks to Our Lady of Grace Under Pressure Cemetery on Cemetery Road. At the cemetery the procession of a dozen cars, lead by the U-Haul hearse, took a left turn at block 17-B, when they should have taken a right, and ended up stuck at a dead-end by the War Dead Memorial. One-by-one the cars had to back out of the corner they were wedged in. With a wide disparity of reversing talent among the respective drivers, not all graves were spared desecration by turns made too wide or too tight. Though, thankfully, and not by much, no headstones were upended entirely, only adjusted on their bases slightly by the reverse procession.

Between the stumbled through mass and the cemetery traffic jam, Father Lucious was late for the start of Melvin Goolie's funeral mass back at Our Lady of Perpetual Suffering by at least ten minutes by the time they had KC's KC-less casket resting on planks over the hole dug fresh that morning just for him. The plot, between KC's father and KC's grandmother, under an overly pruned maple, had been reserved for KC's mother, but, she figured, KC needed it more than she did at the moment. Besides, the nearest available plot was on the far side of the cemetery, in the newly opened section that looked like a soccer field, and a mid-field plot cost nearly $1,500.

In a rush, and unencumbered by muttered aloud rosaries, Father Lucious flew through the internment rites. Not taking a breath through the entire dust-to-dust-ashes-to-ashes bit. When time to do so, he swung the incense thurible with such manic vigour that a thick black cloud of smoke engulfed the gravesite, choking the mourners, throwing several into serious, prolonged coughing fits, including those nearest the grave: KC's mother;

KC's pallbearers—KC's uncle Randy, KC's cousins Charlie, Larry, Louis, and Gino, and KC's best-friend Morton; the eleven-year-old altar boy, Rory, and Father Lucious himself.

Once the cloud of thick incense smoke had settled and the coughing had subsided, Father Lucious took a long, polished brass, cylindrical container from his pocket, unscrewed the lid, and poured charcoal ash in the shape of a cross on the lid of the casket in roughly the spot KC's head would be, were KC's head there at all, while hurriedly repeating the dust-to-dust-ashes-to-ashes bit in his tourist phrasebook Latin. The charcoal ash cross was the cue for the two gravediggers, one named Graves—no joke—and the other named Ernst, both in matching work boots and dull green coveralls, both caked in the grey-brown-orange dirt from KC's grave, both carrying long steel jack handles, to emerge from seemingly nowhere (actually from behind the backhoe parked a respectable distance from the grave, where they had been smoking cigarettes and talking about hockey and women throughout the entirety of the internment ceremony). They politely excused themselves through the crowd, shooing the mourners to either end of the grave so they could remove the planks from beneath KC's casket. With the planks removed— though, not without some difficulty, one of the more ornery planks required Ernst to push the casket nearly over on its side, with his heavy, dirty, work boot, to create enough space to free the plank—Graves and Ernst inserted their long steel jack handles into the appropriate orifices of the casket-lowering apparatus, which was suspending KC's casket over his grave with two seatbelt-width green straps, and began cranking what was left of KC into the ground.

The thick black incense smoke from Father Lucious' over-zealous thurible, however, had left a coarse soot covering the polished brass casket-lowering apparatus. As Graves and Ernst cranked, some of this soot worked its way into the works of the apparatus, jamming the gears on the foot-end. Graves, at the head-end, continued cranking while Ernst, on the foot, leaned his not-inconsiderable heft on the end of his long steel jack handle, without success. By the time Ernst had quietly gotten Graves' attention and got him to stop cranking until the jammed foot gear problem could be sorted, much of Father Lucious' charcoal ash cross he'd left on the lid of the casket in roughly the spot KC's head would be, were KC's head there at all, had slid off the casket lid and wafted gently into the darkness below. All that remained of the cross was a dusty smudge on the Alice-blue casket.

Graves left his post at the head to add his also not-inconsiderable heft to the end of Ernst's long steel jack handle. The casket-lowering apparatus creaked and moaned under the collective not-inconsiderable heft of Graves and Ernst. Creak and moan. Moan and creak.

All at once a loud shot rang out and Graves and Ernst collapsed in a pile, Ernst atop Graves. As the casket-lowering apparatus buckled, KC's KC-less casket gave a wild buck and pitched violently foot-downward, slipped from the casket-lowering apparatus's two seatbelt-width green straps, and plunged the final five feet into the blackness of the grave, landing with a hollow thud on the bottom. The casket landed on a face-down angle so that, being roughly the same length as the grave was deep, the bottom corner of the head-end, where the back of KC's head would be, were KC's head there at all, was level with the surface. The violence of the tumble jarred open the lid of KC's casket, spilling its contents into the bottom of the grave.

The foremost mourners, including KC's mother, KC's pallbearers—KC's uncle Randy, KC's cousins Charlie, Larry, Louis, and Gino, and KC's best-friend Morton—Father Lucious and his eleven-year-old altar boy, Rory, and the two grave-diggers, Graves and Ernst, collected themselves and leaned over KC's open grave to survey the wreckage of KC's casket. Slumped in the bottom foot-end of the grave, spilled from the casket, was a deceased elderly gentleman, perhaps in his eighties, in a nice navy blue suit.

A Drawer full of Guggums

Sharon Bala

D OROTHEA'S MOTHER HAD been a fan of George Eliot. I was named for the foolish girl who chose the wrong husband, she said. Dodo. Call me Auntie Do.

Cait sat, upright and uncomfortable, on the very edge of the armchair. The stranger, who she must now remember to call Auntie Do, sat across from her on the love seat. She was a shrunken woman with the limbs of a bird and brown skin like worn leather. A rice belly muffined out from beneath her sari. She wore a cardigan (correction: jumper). Her hair was plaited and hung over one shoulder.

At the door, she had repeated Cait's name like a foreign word. Cait-lyn. This is your name?

And Cait had felt awkward, not quite annoyed. Then it occurred to her that she was expected to have a traditional name.

Saraswati after the goddess or something unpronounceable like Mangaiyarkarasi.

When Cait said she was from Vancouver, Do quizzed her about Simon Fraser University. Cait had graduated from the University of British Columbia four months earlier. She hadn't realized SFU had international street cred.

Do brought out tea on a silver tray. The cups and saucers were delicate. They made Cait feel like she too might be a character dreamed up by George Eliot. The saucer lay cold in her left palm as if it had just come out of the fridge; the cup was hot. Princess Diana smiled shyly out of a circle of ivy, head tilted in one direction, eyes slanting in the other. *Dodo.* Cait had an intense urge to laugh. She made Diana face away and then there was Charles, ears like a trophy.

Do asked about her studies and Cait explained about the Pre-Raphaelites.

Ah, ah...these pictures with the knights and ladies.

Cait knew she was thinking of the wrong paintings but the flat was in London proper and it didn't seem worth it to correct her. They were sizing each other up and Cait was catching glimpses, trying to knit them all together into some kind of gestalt. A flowered love seat, not even a full-sized sofa. A gorgeous Victorian fireplace, all bricked-in. The walls were covered in cross-stitch. Stick figures kicking up their heels glared at Cait, giving her the stink eye. Do had moved to London in 1958. Forty-four years and not a single photograph.

For two hundred pounds less, Do said Cait could share the master bedroom. The room was dim and suffused with a fragrance Cait associated with Sri Lankan aunties of a certain age, a quaint perfume, cheap but inoffensive. There was a double bed with a pink coverlet and, inches away, a narrow single—light blue sheets with hospital-crisp corners. Cait filed it all away for later, an amusing anecdote to email home.

I really need a desk, she said. Can I see the other room?

There were no rubbish bins in the London Underground. A collection of tissues and Orbit wrappers accumulated in Cait's pocket. She got a job filing papers at the Tate and another washing dishes at a pub close to Do's flat.

Between work and classes, she studied in a vacuum-sealed reading room at the British Library. It was a terrifying place with a deficit of oxygen and an imposing domed ceiling. People were constantly nodding off, then jerking awake to glance around, sheepish.

It was a room that bullied you into hard work. Sitting in an uncomfortable ugly green chair, the cursor blinking on the blank page of her document, Cait felt the whole long history of British scholarship and the weight of its responsibility.

She had come to England to research the mercurial genius Dante Gabriel Rossetti, but had fallen under the spell of his melancholy mistress, Lizzie Siddal. Lizzie worked in a hat shop off Leicester Square when they met. Rossetti said she was his destiny, that they had been doomed lovers in a previous life. They read Tennyson out loud by candlelight and called each other Guggum.

Guggum. Cait said the word then couldn't stop laughing. Every face in the reading room scowled in her direction.

Lizzie was a stunner and all the artists wanted her to model for their paintings. Her hair was long and loose, unlucky red.

Cait grew her own hair long. She let the natural waves come out, then pinned them all up away from her ears so they would cascade down late-nineteenth-century style. She grew fascinated by the word languorous, the way the vowels tumbled over each other, and repeated it to herself over and over.

Other words came back to her. She would wake up and her first thoughts would be in Tamil—the word for butterfly or blue materializing. She had once, as a child, been entirely fluent but now she could comprehend but not speak—remember, the word door, say, but never recall the verb to go. When Do spoke Tamil her voice jangled like bangles on a wrist. The language limped back to Cait, like an atrophied muscle reawakened after a coma.

When I came to London, a loaf of bread was five pence, Do said.

She arranged a plate and a water glass on a placemat as Cait pulled out a chair. Do sat across the table and watched Cait spoon dhal onto her plate. She made her dhal the way Cait liked it—

thick and substantial, speckled with mustard seeds. The deal was room and half-board: breakfast and three curries for dinner. Cait never saw Do eat.

It was Friday, a vegetarian day. There were string hoppers and pol sambol made with fresh coconut that Cait had scraped that morning, one hand on the hairy brown shell and the other turning the crank, listening to the blades grate against the cored-out husk. She'd left the coconut halves on the counter, one on top of the other like helmets, and a mound of white flakes on a plate.

You moved to London alone? Cait asked.

Yes, yes, Do said. I knew only my husband.

So there had been a husband. Cait pulled apart the spider-web hopper, gathering a little pile of stringy noodles, dhal, and sambol in one hand. Turmeric stained her fingers yellow. The first mouthful had a satisfying capsicum burn.

Do had a bottle of baby oil—Johnson & Johnson, clear with a pink cap. The top corner of the label had peeled away and folded in on itself. Do flicked the lid up with her thumb. She poured oil onto her palm then rubbed it into her hair, root to tip until it looked wet.

Selva was taking a chemistry degree, Do said. At the University of London, same place you're studying. I was a young girl then, your age. I had never seen so many white people.

To Cait, London was not especially white-washed. It might have been Vancouver—full of dark faces, lidless almond eyes, accents from the farthest colonial outposts.

Did you meet your husband in Sri Lanka? Cait asked. She never saw Do knitting booties. No one phoned on Sundays.

Do sectioned her hair into thirds and began to form a plait. She said, Yes, in Ceylon, but he was already studying here by then. Selva was so intelligent. She did the side-to-side head bob thing Cait had never mastered. And handsome, Do said. All my sisters were jealous when he chose me. They were a little big made. Do puffed out her cheeks as she said this and Cait imagined three portly sisters, saris billowing on the couch. Like something out of Austen.

Do tied the end of her braid into a knot and tossed it over her shoulder. I was slim in those days, she said. And fair, like you.

This crazy obsession with light skin when they were naturally disposed to being dark! Cait was glad her mother didn't go in for any of that nonsense. It is because you put cream on your face, Do liked to say. Cait didn't tell her the "cream" was foundation.

Do stood up. Tomorrow, I'll make kothu. She stroked Cait's hair as she left the table. Cait closed her eyes and felt the pressure of Do's hand on the back of her head. She missed her mother. Take some more, Do said. Sappida. Eat.

How come we never speak Tamil? Cait asked her father that night, during a rare transatlantic call.

Because we're Canadian, he said. If you want, we can speak in French.

My Tamil is an embarrassment, her mother said, on the other extension. It's been too long.

This from the woman who had never bothered to learn the word broom and instead called it a sweeper.

They wanted to know about her cousin. Have you seen Nisha yet?

Ask me in Tamil, Cait said.

You've gone to England to become more Sri Lankan, her father said. Watch you don't pick up the wrong accent.

Cait held the phone away from her ear. Her father still thought of overseas calls as happening in 1977.

The carpet was being replaced and Cait was stuck in the flat, listening to the builders bang about, because Do was terrified of being alone with them.

But I'm a stranger too, Cait wanted to say. You let strangers sleep in your room!

Imagine living your whole life as if one's neighbours were foreigners.

Cait's desk was covered in photocopies, hardcovers, and open notebooks. She was hunched over an exhibition guide she had borrowed from the museum, glossy pages bearing full-colour reproductions of Pre-Raphaelite paintings.

Lizzie had modelled for Ophelia. She'd floated, uncomplaining, in a tub of ice-cold water then caught pneumonia. Eyes half-closed, lips slightly parted, hands held out, Lizzie's Ophelia was ethereal, a suicidal martyr.

Do's head materialized in the doorway. She wore a cotton sari and a coat over top. Her blinding white trainers were already laced up. She made a furtive gesture, palm down, fingers pulling at the air in two quick scoops. Come, come, she said.

The drills and hammers were going hard in the lounge. A giant plastic sheet hung in front of the closed door. Cait and Do stood whispering in the hallway.

What's wrong? Cait asked.

I'm going to Sainsbury's, Do said. Stay here and watch them.

Here? Cait thought. In the hallway, like a spy?

She'd answered the doorbell that morning, Do cowering behind. There were two men in blue-jean coveralls. They brought their lunches in organ transplant cooler boxes and asked if it would be okay to use the microwave later.

What am I watching for? Cait asked.

Make sure they don't get up to any funny business, Do said, reaching for her grocery cart.

After Do left, Cait thought she had better offer the men some tea. They asked for PG Tips with plenty of milk.

Cait leaned against the kitchen counter and read while she waited for the water to boil. Rossetti couldn't bear the thought of sharing, so Lizzie began to model for him exclusively. He was the first to recognize her talent and took her on as a pupil.

The grout between the countertop tiles was crumbled with morning toast. Cait rolled a finger over a bit of rye and flattened the book covers down with her elbow as she read.

When Lizzie's paintings didn't sell, Rossetti wrote limericks to cheer her up, rhyming her name with tizzy and frizzy. Cait's lips sounded out the poems mutely. She felt maternal and fond.

The phone in the kitchen was fire-engine red with a kinked up cord and a rotary dial face. Its high-pitched ringtone startled her, annoyed, out of the nineteenth century.

A man asked for Do. He called her Mrs. Selvarajah. At first Cait thought the caller was her father but then the disembodied voice demanded: Who are you?

Hey! Cait said. You're the one who called here. She felt bold, on the safe end of the theatre-prop telephone.

May I ask when she's due back? he said, at once haughty and polite.

Cait tried to match a face to the diluted, familiar accent. Leave your name and I'll tell her you rang, she said.

Water bubbled in the window of the plastic plug-in kettle. Steam rose from the spout.

Is she coming home today?

That's none of your business! Cait slammed the receiver onto the cradle.

She brought the builders their tea and tried to make small talk but they had impossible Geordie accents and all she could

think about was double-checking the locks. Who did that rude
caller think he was—asking such intrusive questions?

By the time Do came home, the men were grunting in the
bathroom. She hovered in Cait's doorway with her hands on her
head.

Aiyo! she said. Big noise!

Cait had decided there was no point telling Do about the
call. It was probably a telemarketer. She felt chagrined now by her
overreaction and regretted the melodramatic hang-up.

She raised her voice over the hammers: No funny business.
She waited, then added, Come in.

An eight-by-eleven print was propped against the wall, one
of Lizzie's watercolours that Cait had found in a charity shop
for fifty pence. Do picked it up, holding the bottom corner
with a thumb and index finger. The paper was stiff; it held itself
up.

A group of women and children huddled together on the
beach, watching for a ship that would never come. The painting
had a smudged quality, as if coloured in with pastels.

It's called *The Ladies' Lament*. Cait pointed. That's the artist.

Lizzie had painted herself as the only standing figure, upright
and stiff, braced for impact.

It is a true story? Do asked.

It's based on a ballad about a shipwreck. This is the moment
the women realize what's happened.

So sad. Do's glasses hung from a string around her neck. When she put them on, they sat huge and plastic, dwarfing her whole face. Do said, Their husbands are not coming back. She nodded to herself.

Do's nails were jagged, in need of a trim. The hand holding the print was arthritic and claw-like. This lady artist, she said. Was she very famous?

Not for her art. She died pretty young.

Do tilted her head left and right, peering at the image from different angles. Cait waited.

I was also young when I lost my husband, Do said.

Somehow Cait had already known this. Whenever she pictured Selva, he was always in his twenties. Shy and studious, he wore his hair parted down the middle and had John Lennon glasses.

He was taken from me, Do said. As if Shiva or a demon had absconded with him in the night.

Cait imagined him walking in the front door with daisies in cellophane. He hugged his bride from behind as she washed the dishes.

From down the hall, the builders conferred with each other in shouts. The drill was a shrieking banshee. Cait pictured a white van clipping a corner, Selva looking left instead of right.

Well I think it was brave of you to stay, Cait said. If it was me, I'd have packed it in and gone straight home.

Do took off her glasses. She put the print down and turned

away from the desk. What to do? I chose England. Only option was to stay.

Do had a subscription to *News of the World*.

They found that poor girl's body, she said. Aiyo!

Cait poured boiling water into the Bodum. She watched steam settle against the glass. Coffee grounds hurricaned around her spoon. Do sat at the table with the tabloid spread out in front of her. She followed the newsprint with a crooked finger.

Cait pressed the plunger down, trapping the coffee grounds, and made a non-committal noise.

That child from Oxfordshire, Do said. They found her in the woods. No clothes. Rape.

There was something unseemly about hearing the word rape come out of Do's mouth. Like seeing one's grandmother naked.

Cait twisted the cap on her travel mug. Okay, Auntie. I'm off.

Do looked up. Without eating?

I had toast.

Do held a banana by the stem and said, Take it. She followed Cait into the hallway, the open newspaper hiding half her body, and read: Identification was made using dental records. The body was found five miles from the family's home in Headington.

Cait bent to zip up her boots. Auntie, she said. I'm going to be late.

Be careful, Do said. Stay on the main road. Don't go in all

these lonely, lonely alleys. Don't take short cuts, especially at night. Not safe in this city.

Waiting at the crosswalk, Cait felt the trains vibrating under her feet. Her head was full of dental records; corpses lurked, decomposing and naked, in autumn leaves. No wonder Do was terrified of strangers. She spent her whole life peering through peep holes and keeping vigil between curtains.

What are you looking at? Cait had once asked.

Nothing. Just to make sure.

Make sure of what? Cait wondered. Do's behaviour reminded Cait of an old family pet—a neurotic Jack Russell with the pretensions of a guard dog, all fifteen pounds at the ready to bark with moral indignation at unsuspecting cats and joggers.

On Fulham Road, Cait thought about Lizzie passing under the same awnings, past the same brown brick facades. The sky hung low and close, a milky white. Fried batter wafted out of the chippy. Lizzie's London would have smelled like effluent and industry, chimneys belching coal smoke, the air thick as pea soup.

Cait walked behind a trio—a tall man with a pony tail and two little girls in navy pinafores and matching rucksacks. She glanced down as she stepped off the curb. Lizzie would have done the same and also raised her skirts. In Southwark, where Lizzie grew up, tailings from the butcher ran bloody over the paving stones. As a child she was doted on by a neighbour called Greenacre, a giant of a man who hoisted her up on his shoulders and sang as he ferried her across the filthy streets.

Cait's supervisor was not happy about the direction of her research. Siddal only sold one painting, he'd said at their last meeting. There's very little scholarship.

All the more reason to research her, Cait said.

Humphreys had to be closing in on seventy. He removed his spectacles and rubbed his small, mole eyes. It's only an MA, he had said. Don't be a hero.

In movies, the heroine moves to a new place and is immediately recruited into a circle of quirky locals. Cait sat in lectures, surrounded by cliques that seemed to have arrived ready-made, as if there was a secret friend lottery she'd neglected to put her name in.

Cait sidestepped a homeless man with a Brillo-pad beard hawking a *Big Issue*. Offal trailed out of a rubbish bin. Homesickness was a palpable thing. It had the texture of failure.

Greenacre was hung for killing his fiancée. He hid her body parts all over London, a scavenger hunt for the police. The story made Lizzie morbid. Years later, she would ruminate on the sordid details, how he had sawn off the woman's arms and legs before he killed her. How all this had happened steps from her home, while Lizzie and her sisters gossiped and darned stockings.

At the Hole in the Wall, Cait glanced around quickly before cupping a hand over the keypad. Do's voice in her ear: They found her in the woods. No clothes. Rape. The machine beeped and her bank card slid out of the slit like a mocking tongue. A body sidled up, warm and foreign. Cait screamed, a harsh, ungainly sound, and spun around, clutching her card and a fist of twenty-pound notes. She looked down and saw a gypsy girl, her dirty brown hand held out. The stranger looked terrified. She couldn't have been more than nine. Cait pressed a twenty into the girl's hands and stammered: You shouldn't...heart attack...

As she hurried toward the Tube station, she passed the father and his twin daughters. The girls were giggling.

Minor surgery was all Do would say. Varicose veins, Cait privately guessed. Appendix? Do walked in and out of rooms, picking up items, putting them down. She straightened the tablecloth, closed the curtain in the lounge, opened it again. She would be in hospital for the weekend. Just a small, small operation, she said, buttoning up her coat.

A biopsy, Cait thought. Her favourite uncle had had a biopsy once. They buried him six months later.

Ah! I've forgotten my baby oil, Do said.

It was half six and Cait's cousin Nisha was arriving from Bristol in an hour. They were spending the weekend together and had the flat to themselves.

Cait picked up Do's carpetbag. Why don't I go with you, Auntie?

The hospital smelled of sickness and bleach. Cait stood in the hallway, watching a porter roll an empty wheelchair. At the nurses' station, a doctor in a white coat stood with her hands on the small of her back, leaning on her heels, and said, Phillipa, how is Mrs. Murphy's BP this evening? Her accent was like shards of glass.

For ten years, Rossetti courted her, inconstant, and Lizzie grew wan with waiting, a tight coil of suspicion whenever he was out of sight. She refused to eat, made herself sick, and he would abandon everything—paid commissions, other women, his father's funeral—when summoned to her bedside. At Hastings, at Bath, at Sheffield, he thought he would lose her, again and again.

The surgeon patted Cait's shoulder when he came out of Do's room. Gall bladder removal, he said. Routine surgery. No reason at all for your granny to worry.

Okay, Cait said. Thank you.

Her relief was deflating. Typical Do: brewing tempests in tea cups.

Do sat up in bed with the sheets tucked around her. She wore a cotton nightgown and her jumper on top. She looked odd and out of place surrounded by an unhooked IV stand and silent heart monitor.

Do you want your cross-stitch? Cait asked.

Do's bag sat unopened on a visitor's chair. Her purse was on the moveable table where her meals would be laid out in their divided plastic containers.

No, no. Nothing. Do turned her hands around each other, as if she was cold. They made a swish, swish sound.

Cait wondered if she should move the bag and sit down, then decided if she did that, she'd never get out.

What time is the surgery? she asked.

Seven in the morning. So early. So early.

You should sleep, Cait said.

Do didn't say anything. She rubbed her hands and stared at the wall. Cait patted her bony shoulder, as the surgeon had done. Do's dark eyes were greying like her hair. Cataracts. Cait had never noticed before. She started to lean closer, then put her hand in her pocket and stepped away. If Selva was here, he would know what to say.

The surgeon seems nice, Cait said. He said there's nothing to worry about.

Yes, yes. Nothing to worry.

Cait zipped up her coat. She took her time putting on her hat, turning up her collar. Her travel card was in her pocket. She took it out and held it in one hand. Do still wasn't looking at her.

I'll see you on Sunday, Cait said. She thought about patting Do's shoulder again or squeezing her hand but didn't. She said, I'm sure everything will be fine.

In the hallway, she walked quickly, eyes on the shiny linoleum, and nearly collided with a nurse stepping off the elevator.

Do you ever feel like they're watching you? Nisha's nose was an inch away from a cross-stitch in a circular frame. A line of pixelated Morris Dancers did high kicks, sticks held over their heads.

Right? Cait said. I swear those beady eyes follow me everywhere.

Nisha reached up and took the hoop off the wall. She turned the dancers around so their backs were on display, the crisscrossed mess of stitches and threads.

Better, Nisha said. So, what's she like then, your Auntie Do?

Cait thought for a moment. She's terrified of black men.

Gawd! Nisha said. Why are immigrants so racist?

Cait gave her a tour of the flat. Nisha walked into Do's room, hands on hips and looked down at the single bed. Who would sleep here?

Do you think anyone actually did?

Nisha was deep into the room, picking through the things on the dressing table. Someone must have, she said. Desperate soul. She uncapped a bottle of perfume and sniffed then set it down beside the baby oil.

Cait hovered in the doorway.

She's not looking for someone to take the bed now, is she? Nisha asked.

A girl came to see the flat ages ago—a student from China—but she never returned.

Nisha made a duck-face in the mirror. She flopped onto Do's

bed, flat on her back. What's it like, I wonder? Come on.

Cait crossed the threshold. She arranged herself on the single, folding her hands across her stomach. Nisha fake snored, imitating her father, making a wet, rumbling sound in her throat.

What time is it? Cait asked. We should get ready.

It's mad! Nisha said. Imagine bunking down with a doddering old stranger.

She's not so bad, Cait said. She stared at the ceiling, divining meaning in the cracks.

Does she talk in her sleep? Nisha asked.

No, Cait lied. It rarely startled her anymore, when Do yelled in her sleep, in a mangled-up Tamil that Cait couldn't decipher.

And what if she sleepwalked! Nisha sat up, eyes closed, arms held out like Frankenstein. Imagine she sleepwalked right into your bed! She jumped in beside Cait and they went tumbling, tickling each other like they used to do as children.

Seriously, Cait, Nisha said, catching her breath. Do you like it here?

What do you mean?

They lay on their sides, mirror imaging each other.

You've been here two months, Nisha said. I thought you'd be getting out more, seeing all of London.

London's a big place.

Cait didn't say that she had no one to explore it with.

All you ever talk about is work and school, Nisha said.

I like work and school. Cait told her about the Guggums.

The British Library! Nisha said. They'll revoke your pass if they think you're having any fun.

Cait rolled onto her back. He used to repeat her name as he painted, she said. Guggum. Guggum. Guggum. Cait heard how stupid the word sounded. She wished she hadn't brought it up; she wasn't doing the story justice. She said, I know it sounds ridiculous but don't you think it's sweet?

But Cait, Nisha said. Wasn't Rossetti a complete pig?

He buried a book of his poetry with her, Cait said. His only copy.

Fine time to grow a conscience. Nisha propped herself up on an elbow. Listen, she said. Colin Firth is in a show at the Old Vic. Promise me you'll see it.

I don't know, things are so busy right now. Cait couldn't admit the truth: that she didn't want to go alone. A passing thought: could she take Do with her? No, definitely not.

Mr. Darcy in spitting distance, Nisha said, holding out a finger. Pinky swear.

Cait hooked fingers. I wish you lived here.

Me too, Nisha said. This last year of uni is doing my head in. She rolled off the bed. Enough faffing about. Let's go dancing. I'm going to show you what you're missing. She ran out of the room, pumping her fists in the air like an American cheerleader and yelling: London-town!

When Nisha was in the bathroom, Cait straightened out both beds, still thinking about the Guggums. Lizzie drank laudanum by the spoonful and Rossetti boasted about his other models. She left a note when she died and he drew sketch after sketch. A drawer full of Guggums.

The phone rang and she picked up the extension on Do's bedside table.

It was the stranger again. Are you her niece? he asked. The question made Cait feel like an interloper, as if she had no business being there.

Sod off, she said and hung up. If the phone rang again, she wasn't going to answer.

Guggum. Guggum. Guggum. She repeated the word in a whisper until it began to sound right again.

In Bloomsbury there were spiked iron fences around the parks and Georgian townhouse blocks, their windows stacked up in neat lines, a fan of glass above each glossy blue door. We are respectable and bourgeois, the houses said. We only drink single malt.

Cait had spent the evening at the British Library, skimming old correspondence and journals. She'd stumbled on a diary entry by Rossetti's sister who'd gone to visit his studio and found it papered with sketches of Lizzie. *Rossetti is everyday with his sweetheart of whom he is more foolishly fond.*

The moon drifted in and out of sight, hidden behind the

clouds. *Foolishly fond.* Cait repeated the line to herself as she walked, full of satisfaction, a solid day of research come to a close. Cutting diagonals through the laneways, she felt like a local. The weekend before, she'd taken Nisha's advice and bought a matinee ticket. She'd sat by herself in a row full of strangers and been thrilled by Colin Firth's proximity, the unadulterated crispness of his voice. Afterward, she'd gone to the Southbank Christmas market, eaten curry wurst out of a paper doily in dainty bites and waved to the children on the carousel while Big Ben chimed six. She'd drunk a bit too much mulled wine and felt quietly exuberant on the Tube ride home.

This is what Cait was learning: In London it was possible to be alone and not lonely. She had taken to navigating without a map and felt intrepid and brave even though she knew she wasn't.

Bloomsbury Square to Great Russell Street. The British Museum. Too far north. She heard the footsteps of the person behind her as she doubled back, sneakers lethargic against pavement, and an ambulance in the distance. There were wreaths hung on doors. Through the windows, she caught glimpses of stockings on mantles and twinkling Christmas trees. Fog blurred the lamplight. Jack Ripper's London.

The thought of Do, anxious at the front window, made Cait feel defiant. A Mini parallel parked between two Peugeots. The bumpers kissed and the driver jumped out, engine still running, to scrutinize the damage. At the street light, a man in a suit, trouser leg tucked into a sock, balanced on a cycle. Two women jogged past, Lycra and reflective tape, and then for a long stretch, she was alone.

Cait veered onto a street that was walled in on both sides. She'd taken a wrong turn somewhere. Everything was still except the footfalls behind her, the same lazy rhythm as before. The street name at the corner was one she didn't recognize. Cait reached into her pocket and held onto her keys, forming her hand into a fist with the biggest key sticking out between two fingers. She told herself: don't panic.

High Holborn was nearby. North or south? She listened for traffic or pedestrian voices, but all she heard were two sets of footsteps. She walked a little faster. With purpose, as *Cosmo* had taught her. She swung her arms. The back of her neck burned. She took stock. She was wearing a pea coat. A belt. Jeans with buttons not a zipper. Okay. She mustn't freak out. She mustn't look back. Did the footsteps have a gender? Possibly it was a granny with a head scarf.

She heard a whistle and a rabble of voices up ahead. Yes, the High Street must be just around this corner. The blood in her ears was the sound of her own panic. If she could just get to a crowded place…. She turned left into a deserted alleyway and then it was too late.

Don't be stupid, she told herself instead of running. London is safe. The alley was long and narrow, pedestrian-only, between two brick buildings. There was a skip, big enough to dump a body, and a tiny verge on one side. Cigarette butts littered the ground. A sleeping bag was bundled inside a cardboard box.

Cait picked up her pace and told herself not to make a spectacle. A handful of fur blurred across her path and she gasped. The fur squeezed through a sewer grate and was gone. She pulled up short, hand on her chest, catching her breath. The voices she had heard came from a window up above. The slosh and clink of pint glasses, jeering footie fans.

A hand circled her bicep. Not a man. Not Jack the Ripper. A boy. A yob. Thin and gangly, still growing into his limbs. His jeans hung low. He urged her backward and she felt her hair catch on the brick wall. His movements were slow and deliberate, without violence.

The boy's face was erupting, angry red acne spilling down his neck. He held her arms at her sides. His grip was firm. Cait's key was still in her fist, pointed down and futile. He wore a baseball cap and a hooded sweatshirt, no jacket. Wasn't he cold? Cait could hear the double-deckers on High Holborn. One of his legs was between both of hers. Fog gathered ghostly around their feet. He smelled of Axe body spray. He wasn't a hobo or a vagrant or a gypsy. His mother bought his underpants at Marks and Sparks. He was pressed up so close she could feel his erection, the spikey whiteheads as his cheek grazed hers. She turned away and his tongue lapped her ear in a single wet stroke. Arsenal scored and the crowd upstairs bellowed their approval.

Cait started to shake. She cried silently, tears streaming down her cheeks. No, no. Please, no. There was pandemonium in her stomach, adrenaline and cortisol rushing in, running back and forth with their hands on their heads. Aiyo! Aiyo!

Something else she recalled from *Cosmo*: shit your pants to scare off a rapist. She couldn't even squeeze out a bit of pee. The boy nuzzled her neck, inching toward her mouth. His breath was warm. He had been sucking a Life Saver. Cherry.

Scream! She had to scream. She struggled to expel a shout. Her voice came out in a yelp: I'm on my period!

A couple stumbled into the far end of the alleyway. They turned to gawk and crash landed into the skip.

George! the girl squealed. You're such a muppet!

The yob released Cait's arms and stepped away in the same fluid movement. He flicked his hood over his cap, and head down, hands in his pockets, sauntered away. Cait went limp against the wall. The back of her fist jammed hard in her mouth. She couldn't stop shaking. The drunk couple, still mauling each other, fell out of the alley, and Cait was alone with the sound of her voice, ugly and embarrassing, echoing in her ears.

Rossetti went mad. He sank into a haze of chloral and whisky, spending his last days as a recluse. He claimed Lizzie's soul was not at peace, that her ghost came to him at night.

An unscrupulous agent convinced Rossetti to publish the

buried poems. They went to the cemetery at midnight, firelight glinting off the blades of their shovels.

Cait sat on the floor with her computer on the coffee table. There were three unanswered emails from Nisha in her inbox. Turning down evening shifts and glancing over her shoulder on major thoroughfares, Cait felt the boundaries of her life closing in. Do had been right all along. Cait understood now that fear was a gift.

She transcribed her research notes and thought of Selva. In Do's wardrobe, under her bed, somewhere in this flat, there must be a shoebox. Love letters, round spectacles, an obituary. Maybe even a news report. Selva was the victim of a hit and run on Tottenham Court Road. Or a fatal mugging in Brixton. Cait had a bubbling-up feeling, the same one she'd had when she recognized Lizzie's brushwork at the charity shop. *Selva was taken from me.* Cait summoned Google.

The man in the picture was corpulent and balding. He'd received a teaching award. Cait heard the metal scrape of a key in the lock. The article included a family photo. A freckled child with frizzy hair held her grandfather's hand. The tongue of the lock retracted with a click. I'd like to thank my wife—my rock for the past forty-three years. The front door swung forward.

Aiyo! Do said. Very cold, very cold. How cold is it in Canada? Like this?

Colder, Cait said, glancing over the top of the computer.

Minus twenty or twenty-five, in some parts.

In the picture, Selva's wife had the look of a woman who laughed with her whole body. Her skin had been ruined by the sun. She'd probably never threaded a needle in her life, this badly preserved ginger, an unlikely Selvarajah.

Do stamped her feet on the mat even though it hadn't snowed. She wore the toque Cait had given her for Christmas two months earlier. Half her face was hidden in a scarf. Her eyes peered out, small and ferrety.

Ah-nay! How to live like this? The scarf unravelled and fell to the ground. She bent to retrieve it and put a hand on her lower back as she levered herself up.

Cait bookmarked the page. Explorer demanded a name. She called it "Selva" then added a question mark.

Cait shut her laptop. Simon Fraser University. Something about this was familiar.

Do sank into the arm chair. Her bottle of baby oil was within reach.

Cait stood. Let me. Their fingers brushed when the bottle changed hands. I do this all the time for my mom, she said. It was only a white lie.

The oil was slippery in Cait's palm. She rubbed her hands together and a drop trickled down to her wrist, over the horizontal line she always thought of as the seam.

Do's hair, once a fat rope of braid, was thin, petering out at the end. Cait spread her fingers over Do's crown. The action reminded her of a school-bus game, hands mimicking a cracking egg, imaginary yolk dripping down past the ears.

It was said that after death, Lizzie's hair had kept growing, that the coffin overflowed with thick, penny-coloured locks.

Do relaxed against the upholstery. Her eyes closed. Cait felt the thinness of her shoulders, saw the brown fragile scalp.

Cait's mother liked to say, A woman's hair is her crowning glory. Every six weeks a bald gay man named Raimund made her greys disappear. Her father called it witness relocation. He always laughed at his own jokes.

Cait massaged Do's scalp, fingers tracing each bump and hollow. She could smell Do's perfume and the baby-soft scent of the oil. The phone rang as she was beginning a French braid.

Cait weaved and twined, pulling with gentle pressure, as her mother had taught her. Let it go, she said. He'll call back.

Acknowledgements

SHARON BALA: "A Drawer Full of Guggums" Copyright © 2015 Sharon Bala. Printed by permission of the author.

MELISSA BARBEAU: "Holes" Copyright © 2015 Melissa Barbeau. Printed by permission of the author.

JAMIE FITZPATRICK: "Like Jewels" Copyright © 2015 Jamie Fitzpatrick. Printed by permission of the author.

CARRIE IVARDI: "Rescue" Copyright © 2015 Carrie Ivardi. Printed by permission of the author.

MATTHEW LEWIS: "The Jawbone Box" Copyright © 2015 Matthew Lewis. Printed by permission of the author.

JENINA MACGILLIVRAY: "Gorillas" Copyright © 2015 Jenina MacGillivray. Printed by permission of the author.

IAIN MCCURDY: "Crossbeams" Copyright © 2015 Iain McCurdy. Printed by permission of the author.

Contributors

SHARON BALA's short fiction has received three Newfoundland and Labrador Arts & Letters Awards. In 2015 her manuscript *The Boat People* won the Percy Janes First Novel Award. She has stories forthcoming in *The New Quarterly*, *Riddle Fence*, *Grain*, and *Room*.

MELISSA BARBEAU is a writer and an instrumental music teacher. She has published in *Paragon I* and *III*, in *The Cuffer Anthology*, and in the online literary journal *Salty Ink*. She has won Newfoundland and Labrador Arts and Letters Awards for fiction and non-fiction and the Cox and Palmer SPARKS Creative Writing Award. She is currently completing an MA in English at Memorial University. Barbeau lives with her husband and their children in Torbay, but her heart lives in Freshwater, Conception Bay.

JAMIE FITZPATRICK's debut novel, *You Could Believe in Nothing*, is about estranged siblings, departed lovers, St. John's, hockey, drink, and the trouble that ensues when an aging disc jockey gets lonely in his motel room out around the bay. His short memoir, "These Memories Can't Wait: Lies My

Music Told Me," is anthologized in *Becoming Fierce*. His writing has also appeared in *The New Quarterly*, *The Cuffer Anthology*, and *The Newfoundland Quarterly*.

CARRIE IVARDI grew up in Mississauga, Ontario. She graduated in Honours English from Bishop's University in Quebec, having spent several semesters in England and France. Her travels have included tree planting in remote regions across Canada, editing an arts and entertainment magazine in British Columbia, writing for CBC radio in Sudbury, marketing for a major Toronto-based firm, and attending a writers' conference in Iceland. She recently relocated from Thompson, Manitoba, with her husband and three children and is currently working on her Master's in English Literature at Memorial University.

MATTHEW LEWIS was born in Carbonear, Newfoundland. He currently resides in St. John's where he works as a building inspector.

JENINA MACGILLIVRAY is a writer, filmmaker, and musician based in St. John's, her home for the past twenty years. Her recent film *Boarding* premiered at the Atlantic Film Festival, and she is the 2015 winner of the RBC Michelle Jackson emerging filmmaker's award for her short script *The Tour*. "Gorillas" is her first publication.

IAIN MCCURDY is from St. John's. He has won numerous awards for fiction, nonfiction, and poetry, most recently a 2015 Arts and Letters award for creative nonfiction for the essay "{(S)(K)(I)(N)}." He enjoys three-act structure, taking off early, flying by the seat of his pants, and, once every now and again, landing butterside up.

LISA MOORE is the author of the novels *Alligator, Caught,* and *February,* the short-story collections *Degrees of Nakedness* and *Open,* and the stage adaptation of her novel *February.* Moore's first young-adult novel, *Flannery,* will be published in April 2016. She is a professor of Creative Writing at Memorial University.

MORGAN MURRAY was born and raised near the same backwoods west-central Alberta village (Caroline) as figure-skating legend Kurt Browning. These days he lives, works, plays, writes, and slowly renovates a really old crappy house with his lovely wife in St. John's. In between, he has been a farmer, a rancher, a roustabout, a reporter, a designer, a Tweeter, and a student in Calgary, Prague, Montreal, Chicoutimi, and Paris. "KC Accidental" originally appeared in *The Broken Social Scene Story Project* (Anansi, 2013).

GARY NEWHOOK is a writer from Paradise, Newfoundland, who now resides in Kilbride. His first break was when MUN Drama produced his play *Snails* in 2010 followed by a win in the Statoil Young Playwriting Series. His work has previously appeared in the online publications *Defenestration* and *Every Day Poetry* and on paper in *Ahoy!* and *Paragon.* He is a member of The Port Authority writing group and has a fondness for growing potatoes and being in the woods.

MELANIE OATES is a writer, filmmaker, and costume designer. She's a winner of the Percy Janes First Novel Award and has written and directed four short films (*Get Out, Distance, Bait, There You Are*). She was also the costume designer for the feature films *Cast No Shadow* and *Closet Monster.* In 2014, she co-founded Carrie at Heart Productions Ltd with her producing partner Jess Anderson. Season one of their web-series *The Manor* is set to be released in fall 2015, and they are currently developing their first feature film project, *Scattered and Small*. Mel is a baygirl living in St. John's.

SUSAN SINNOTT has a healthcare background but now spends her time writing fiction. She is a member of The Port Authority writing group, and in 2014 she won The Percy Janes First Novel Award for her manuscript *Just Like Always*. Sinnott lives in St. John's.